The Genesis

The ageless citizens of Homakuwa who evolved from humans in *Sea Species* and *The Envoy* continue their efforts to save the Earth and humanity after the devastating destruction of the environment. With ninety percent of the human population wiped out, civilization is on the brink of extinction. Only the genetic technology of the descendant species, Homakuwa, can bring the ecosystem back before starvation and savagery takes the last humans. The United World Government holds civilization together as they recover, but a new society arises from those left out of the UWG plan. The technology of the past was saved, and a program to use robots for the labor force results in Artificial Intelligence and a new species on Earth. As the caretakers of humanity, can Homakuwa keep the species from extinction at their own hands? In *The Envoy*, Homakuwa expanded beyond Earth designing themselves as space creatures. They began to inhabit the other planets and design themselves for those environs. In an exploratory effort, Homakuwa sends biological starships toward the center of the galaxy. As they spread out into the universe, encountering new collective minds and opening to new dimensions, they become a new species. And the cycle of evolution starts anew.

By R. L. Clayton

The Evolution River Series
Sea Species
The Envoy
The Genesis

The Dead Series
Dead & Dead For Real
Dead Reckoning
Dead Again

Wings of the WASP

Visit R. L. Clayton's website
www.evolutionriver.com
www.rlclaytonbooks.com

Acknowledgements

First, I must thank Alexis Powers, who is my goad and my guru. She prodded me to keep going, advised me on how to write better, and edited my draft. Thank you, and I look forward to collaborating with you on future efforts.

My editor Kathy Morris was invaluable in taking my mere effort and turning it into a real book. Thank you for help in making me a better writer.

I want to thank Teri Vonn and Katharine Nelson for their help in moving this from words into a story worth reading.

And last but not least, I want to thank my wife, Linda, for daring me to finish. Your doubt that I could do this is what I needed, just to show you. You know me so well.

The Genesis takes us eons into the future along the Evolution River. As the familiar characters in the series expand and grow, I felt my own awareness widening to embrace more than my five senses. The logical progression of evolution in this series seems undeniable as to where we–actually our descendants are going. It opened my mind to a universe beyond what we know and took me to the end of evolution. Read on, take the voyage, expand your mind.

Robyn Lester, author of *Origin of an Empath*

Robert Clayton's vision of a future world is filled with amazing technology, as well as an outstanding insight into human nature. The Genesis provides a provocative and intelligent scenario of a possible solution, which will enable humanity to survive.

Alexis Powers, author and columnist.

[Type text]

THE GENESIS

The Genesis

Future History of Human Evolution

Volume 3
The Evolution River Series

Prologue

"More than six BILLION people dead!" Ron Carson said, looking at the representatives, the remaining world leaders around the table. Several gasped. They knew of the casualties in their own countries, but the global statistics were stunning. Ron continued, "Worldwide famine will wipe the rest of us out within two years. The only reason we are here now is because we stockpiled every edible morsel before this disaster, now named the Catastrophe. That food will soon be exhausted. Ninety percent of the plants and animals on Earth are already extinct, and we must find a way to grow food, or we will perish, too." He waited to let the audience digest this update, then continued, his voice softer. "We have a chance to survive, but we must stick together as a civilization with government and laws. Scattering into small bands will ensure our demise." For a moment, Ron gazed out knowing the shock of the near destruction of civilization had numbed them. His job was to jolt them awake and guide them to take action. Ron appeared to be forty-five, his sandy hair touched by gray, his back straight. He was once president of the United States, followed by becoming the first president of the United World Government. None of the humans in the audience were aware of these facts, believing that Ron Carson died decades ago. He was one of the last humans to join the civilization of Homakuwa and gain their longevity.

"Enough doom and gloom. We have brains, technology, and power, but we must keep optimism. The good news is that the Orbiting Power System continues to beam energy to Earth we can receive and use. That power plus our people can bring forth ideas so we can rebuild. But the window of opportunity is small.

"We must reestablish communication within the United World Government, giving them the power to manage. Next, we must become skilled at growing food. Though we live in darkness, power is available to create light. Greenhouses would work, along with a distribution system to deliver the food to the people. Present living quarters are inadequate because of the low temperatures and intense storms. A program to build cities underground must launch immediately. Without creating an ecosystem on Earth, we won't be here much longer. Eventually, our skies will clear and our scorched soil will produce, but not soon enough for us to live as we once did.

"Prejudice and bigotry must be set aside. We need to join hands. Today, we in this room represent the inhabitants of the world, and those inhabitants are not black, white, Asian, European, human or non-human. We are the survivors. We must elect leadership and pull together. We will hold a State of the World announcement soon. Quickly return to your people to assess their situations. Redefine the term 'Dire.'"

PART 1

Chapter One

A tall, slender woman with shoulder-length blonde hair stepped onto the raised dais to address the assembled leaders of the survivors of the Catastrophe on Earth. The auditorium was crowded, with some delegates standing in the rear.

"I am Katharine Levey, the president of the marine nation of Homakuwa, the second native intelligent species to inhabit the Earth. As part of the State of the World message, I present our nation to you. Most of you have vague ideas of what Homakuwa is. I begin with a short history of how we got here."

A holographic view of the rotating Earth seen from space filled the air above the crowd in the arena. The Earth was a beautiful cloud-dotted ball with landmasses and blue seas. The hologram zoomed in on different locations of bustling cities:

Beijing, New York, Paris, London, Mexico City, Sydney, and others. "This is our planet pre-Catastrophe. There were seven billion people living on the Earth. Large cities were the centers of commerce with populations of tens of millions."

Katharine's voice filled the stark silence of the auditorium. "The Catastrophe occurred when a series of meteoroids struck the Earth. The small ones caused little damage, but twenty-three large ones hit the planet. "This is the view from space." The blue planet Earth spun in black space with a starry background. Fiery streaks shot through the atmosphere and rained down. Clouds rose, obscuring the planet. Another scene of a clouded black sky above a barren land and inky sea appeared. "In addition to the meteoroids, the repeated impacts led to instability in the Earth's crust and volcanic eruptions. The giant Icelandic volcano Katla spewed out megatons of ash. Others added to the mayhem." A scene of Katla showed belching clouds rising into the sky, while a maelstrom of lightning bolts danced like demons. "The worldwide firestorm set off by the meteorites created the Dark. Most plant life along with ninety percent of animal life perished." The hologram went dark, and there was silence in the dim auditorium. A spotlight highlighted Katharine.

"I open this meeting with the history of our Earth from before this calamity until now. Those events define who we are today. Though taught in school, the impact of the Catastrophe on Earth's life can only be understood by seeing it. None of you were here during the Catastrophe, or the subsequent years we struggled to survive."

In the darkness above the crowd, a view of blackened and desolate plains filled the air. The smell of smoke seemed to permeate. The woman's voice continued. "This was the surface of our world after the meteorite collisions set off what we now call the Catastrophe and led to mass extinctions. Nearly lifeless, we exist today only because we harvested and stored every scrap of food. That was not enough food to sustain humanity during the years of the Dark. We face an unprecedented situation, and the decisions we make will determine whether Homakuwa and the human race survive. We must work together. Homakuwa has talents and technology to help us overcome the possible annihilation of civilization on Earth.

"The rain of meteoroids darkened our skies taking us into Impact Night. Life was devastated. The loss of plants destroyed the very basis of the food chain. We faced extinction. Only now are we starting to work it out. We, Homakuwa and you, the leaders of the human world, are in a position to direct the structure of life on the surface of the Earth. This will not be a retrofit but a new system as we emerge. There are decisions we need to make regarding universality of humans. Will we again consist of ethnic groups with social systems differing from area to area? Under the United World Government, we moved away from that system, which greatly reduced the friction from culture to culture, but diversity was lost. We are in a position to choose what is next." She looked at the sea of faces. How could they contemplate what their parents and grandparents faced with the loss of everything and everyone?

"One certainty is that we must build and maintain a complete education system that does not end when childhood is over. It is a lifetime task. Even though the education centers are small, the program is huge. The key is that every person has access and availability to an education. A family of four has four com centers. There must be a basic level of instruction mastered by each child. Other curriculums can vary." Some in the audience looked puzzled.

"The Prophet brought uniformity to religion around the world. Faithism does not deal in the minutia of religion, but one's relationship with God. All religions of the world are now variations of Faithism, and the Prophet continues to bring the message to all who will listen. We have the opportunity to make a better world." Katharine stepped back.

A pretty mocha-skinned woman with short black hair stepped forward.

"I am Leticia Gardner, Vice President and Technical Director of Homakuwa. I would like to give you the technical status in Homakuwa today. The Orbiting Power System was built before the Catastrophe to supply clean power to Earth. Using genetic technology, we designed citizens to live in space and operate the OPS. We continue to beam microwave energy to Earth in hopes that enough penetrates the cloud layer to be useful." A hologram appeared above the audience showing the blackness of space surrounding the Earth. A large mirror captured and focused the sunlight. "This is one of our collectors."

The first citizen designed for space life was named Chetnaz. She had a bulbous jellyfish shape with tentacles from all sides, some of which ended in hands. Eyes surrounded her body, even on the tips of tentacles. In the weightlessness of space, she could pull herself around with her hands, or inflate and jet like a balloon. Chetnaz and the other space-designed members of the Tashogith Kihhim (Tohono O'odham for Sun Village) live in Homakuwa habitats throughout the Solar system. She was so alien that no image of her appeared to the humans.

Leticia spoke again. "Chetnaz and other citizens have established colonies and habitats surrounding Earth." The hologram zoomed in on a large cylindrical rock slowly spinning around its long axis. The view inside showed a glowing rod in the center with jungle-like plant life coating the walls. Spidery figures moved within. "This is one of our orbiting habitats. It is self-contained, though the creatures living here are not humanoid."

A murmur passed through the crowd at the view.

"We also built habitats on the moon." The hologram showed the lustrous crater-pocked orb then zoomed in on a cluster of clear bubbles and mirrors. The view switched to a large cavern with a glowing tube down the length. Vegetation filled every space. More creatures scuttled among the plants.

"As we spread through the Solar system, we designed colonies and species for the different environments." The hologram displayed the unmistakable landscape of Mars. In the forefront was a green mass of lichen covering the rocks, and swarms of ant-like insects moving through it. Tumbleweeds moved through the view. "Each environment we've encountered has a unique ecosystem. On Mars, the colony is the entity, not the individuals." The gazes of those in the auditorium were locked onto the hologram.

"Our space transports are also living beings. Some of these are solo ships, like Sylvix, who heroically met the onslaught of meteoroids and diverted those that would have resulted in the total destruction of life on Earth. Others are complete nomadic colonies with an integrated ecosystem of many different life forms."

The hologram displayed another cylindrical rock similar to the habitats orbiting Earth. Large sails surrounded it as it moved toward Saturn. As the view zoomed inside, the vegetation-filled interior also swarmed with a myriad of creatures.

"Always curious, we are launching starships to explore the galaxy. These starships are entities themselves, both solo and nomadic colonies. We are headed toward the center of the galaxy for additional discovery."

There was stunned silence in the auditorium. On Earth, life struggled to survive while Homakuwa grew and expanded. To the humans it didn't seem fair that they were left behind to face the hardships of life on the new Earth. The representatives of Homakuwa noted the hardening expressions of envy.

Chapter Two

Jamie Wong spoke through the mental connection–the Collective mind–shared by the members of Homakuwa, of his efforts over the last two years. "To survive, we had to rebuild life on Earth from the base up, and we had to do it quickly." Physically, Jamie Wong sat with Leticia Gardner and Donald Brown in an underwater chamber. Jamie was short, slightly pudgy, with Asian features. When Homakuwa gained the ability to design life, these descendants of humans became a civilization. This new species is not defined by physical characteristics, but by the ability to create life to thrive within any environment.

The chamber was in the submerged city of Ocealla. The curved walls of the circular room glowed green, supplying only a dim light. One side was transparent, looking out into a dark underwater seascape where a few vague shapes moved. Jamie fumbled with black framed glasses, kept out of choice–his vision had been corrected decades before. These people were the original developers of the genetic technology that defined the civilization of Homakuwa as a new species. They were the descendants of humans, using genes to create life the way humans use wood, plastic, and metal to create things.

Jamie: [Using our technology, we must accelerate the creation of an ecosystem on Earth while it recovers from the Catastrophe. The cataclysmic destruction of the Earth has destroyed the basis of life by shrouding the planet in clouds of dust, smoke, and water vapor blocking out sunlight. When the base of the food chain, plants and algae, died out, everything above that died. To survive, an ecosystem must be established before our food stores run out. That means growing food within two years. Nature doesn't work that fast, so it's up to us.]

The featureless interior of the room was only broken by the chairs, which were one piece with the floor, and a raised open tank in the center of the room. The water in the tank rippled, and a dolphin-like head broke the surface. An amorphous shape rose beside it. There was no sound, but the Collective mind carried the meeting throughout Homakuwa.

Jamie: [The sea is where we started to rebuild. I've designed algae species that live in very low light conditions. Within a year, the dense cover over Earth will begin to thin. We will have twilight.] A view of a gray sky appeared. [In addition, I designed algae able to use the energy beamed from the OPS. These species grow well in low temperature climates. Without predators and with exponential growth, we have established colonies within these two years. Once the bottom of the food chain is reestablished, we can add animals.]

Blue Streak: [What about the surface world?] Blue Streak was an enhanced dolphin created by Jamie Wong. She was the oldest citizen of her kind in Homakuwa.

Leticia: [The Darkness, starvation, the ice age, and disease devastated the human population, killing almost ninety percent. Survivors live in the temperate belt around the equator. The evacuation of the coastal areas to the interior saved more lives than the stored supplies can sustain. Devastating storms are wreaking havoc in the cities. The Orbiting Power System provides energy that keeps these populations alive, but their small greenhouses do not grow adequate provisions.]

Jamie: [The modified mushrooms and other fungi helped, but they are not enough. For humans to survive, we must get plants growing again.]

Unweil: [What about our colonies in Earth orbit? I know they survived the Catastrophe with little damage, and we are expanding throughout the Solar system. Can they help with food for the humans?] Unweil was an underwater Construct of Homakuwa. She was like a squid, but with hands at the end of some of her arms and eyes completely around her body.

Leticia: [The orbiting colonies are self-sufficient ecosystems. To send food to Earth, materials have to be returned for balance. The humans no longer have the capability of launching supplies into space. Whatever mass is sent out must be replenished.]

Katharine Levey broke into the conversation through the mental link. [When will we have viable provisions for the humans?]

Jamie: [It will be at least five years before we establish food fish. The low-level grains I'm growing are not doing well, yet.]

Kit Carson, one of the last humans to become a citizen of Homakuwa entered the conversation. He was a younger version of his great-grandfather, Ron, with a handsome youthful face and light brown hair.

Kit: [I've been listening, and an idea occurred to me. There is power to light greenhouses, but the humans cannot build them fast enough to supply adequate food. Jamie, could we design a biological greenhouse, one that grows instead of being constructed?]

Jamie: [An interesting idea. Let me work on that. It may be possible. I'll get back to you.]

Katharine: [Without something changing quickly, surviving populations must consolidate into smaller groups. We'll lose half of the remaining human population within the next two years. Let's see what we can do. Rich, are you with us?]

Rich: [I'm here, Katharine.] Rich Lewis was the engineer who had designed the original Kihhim and a genius with anything mechanical. He looked the part, slender with thinning hair and glasses. A pocket protector full of pens would not have been out of place though he wore tee shirts now.

Katharine: [Rich, we need to get a crash program going for underground housing. The surface cities are not holding up under the cold and storms. The structures weren't designed for continuous high winds, and the dusts clouds are burying whole buildings. Anything you need just let me know.]

Rich: [Okay, Katharine. A good challenge.]

Leticia: [There is one other thing we must consider. I believe Homakuwa should work from the background. Our humanoid members should integrate into human society, but the rest should fade back. Humans have a history of lashing out at differences during times of stress, and this is stress to the extreme. We should minimize the visibility of our marine habitats and civilization.]

Katharine: [I agree.] There were other assents.

Homakuwa was a civilization that began in a small community near the Tohono O'odham reservation at the foot of Baboquivari Peak in Southern Arizona. They called their community Kihhim, which was the Tohono O'odham word for 'Village'. When Kihhim moved to the ocean, they named themselves Kahchk Kihhim (T.O. for *Sea Village*) and began to genetically design themselves as a marine species.

Members of Kahchk Kihhim had no common physical characteristics but were designed for the environment they inhabited. As Homakuwa continued to grow, they developed a mental connection called the Collective mind. When Homakuwa expanded into space, new species were created for life there. Homakuwa continued its expansion throughout the Solar system, and its citizens are of different sizes and shapes, only a few of them humanoid.

Chapter Three

Sylvix deployed her solar sails like a butterfly emerging from a cocoon. Sylvix was a spaceship, a creation of Jamie Wong and Rich Lewis. Her wings, more than two-thousand square miles in area, captured the solar wind and pushed her outward from the star system of Sol. Using planets and moons as a slingshot, she would reach the edge of the system in five years.

Many of her sister spaceships were transporting members of Homakuwa around the star system of Sol, starting colonies on planets and moons. Others were colony ships, with permanent habitats in space. Sylvix was the first spaceship Homakuwa grew that was an entity itself. She had no passengers and was a bionic being.

Sylvix had been the first to spot the approaching peril of the Catastrophe and tried to divert the meteoroids, but there were too many. She still prevented the destruction of all civilization by deflecting the largest.

With recovery underway on Earth, she and Homakuwa decided to venture beyond the Solar system into the Milky Way galaxy. Sylvix was the first of the explorers, starships and colony ships Homakuwa would dispatch in this venture to learn more about the universe.

Leticia: [Sylvix, you have done so much for us, and humans will forget, but Homakuwa will not. We all look forward to your discoveries.]

Sylvix: [Leticia, I'll be with you in the Collective, at least I hope so. All of the star system of Sol is connected like a single meeting place, but we've never tested it outside the Solar system. Thus far, distance has no effect. Without Homakuwa, this could be a long and lonely voyage.]

Leticia: [Stay with us, Sylvix. Though your body is far away, you are with us.]

Sylvix: [When do you plan to send the other starships and colony ships?]

Leticia: [We're growing and constructing them now. Cyclovix will depart within a year, and we're constructing the colony ships. The first will be inhabited within two years and ready to leave.]

Sylvix: [Is Jamie fine with seeding the star systems with more of us? He wasn't really in favor when we spoke.]

Jamie: [You were right to propose it. When you reach the first system, I'll be ready to help you. We've placed inhabitants in most of the environments in the Solar system, so I'm looking forward to new environs.]

Leticia: [Homakuwa is spreading. We are growing.]

Chapter Four

In the weeks following the Catastrophe, the remnants of the United World Government elected Ron Carson president. The evacuation of the inhabitants from the coastal areas, planned before the meteorite strikes, had shifted huge populations inland. The logistics of maintaining billions of refugees worked for the short term but was unsustainable in the long run.

Ron faced tough decisions before, but no man ever made a judgment of this magnitude. He never regretted the position of president before, always trying to better the world. He hung his head and listened to the people around him. This decision tore at this soul because there was no right answer.

"Mr. President," started the representative from Europe, "More troops are needed to protect our cities." Others in the room raised their voices. "Madrid, Paris and Berlin are in danger of losing to the gangs. The protection has been breached twice, and only because we were able to rush reserves in were they saved. Once the hordes coordinate the attacks, the cities will fall."

"Mr. President, we can send a few troops from Mount Isa," offered the representative from Australia. "No great number of rabble crossed the desert from the other cities. We mobilized the people for protection, too."

"Thank you," said Ron. "Your offer is gratifying. Ladies and gentlemen, most of us are asking for more troops to protect our people. Simply put, we have one fourth of the troops needed to assure the security of camps and cities and to safeguard the supplies. We cannot protect them. We can only feed those in the camps for about another year." The faces in the audience wore grim expressions.

"If nothing is done, everyone in the world is threatened. Without organization, our programs to bring Earth back will disappear. If we fail to find a way to produce food soon, humanity will die out. Pockets may survive but after fifty years, technology will be lost, and within a century, even with clear skies, there won't be sustainable populations. Society will return to the Dark Ages." Ron squelched the trembling inside him at delivering this news. It had to be done.

"When that happens, civilization will be lost. This will be the hardest decision you ever make. Our loyalty must lie with the people of the Earth, not individual countries. Within three days, I will accept nominations for a committee to decide how to allocate resources. From those elected, five will be chosen for this board. The committee's decisions will be final. Let me be clear on this. We must consolidate our populations to numbers we can sustain. That means leaving large numbers of people to perish. This meeting is adjourned until three days from now."

There was silence at the impact of Ron's words. This body of eighty-three must find enough accord to put forth names of those to support their people. The five on the committee would decide the fate of whole countries. They would be responsible for the deaths of millions. The delegates looked at each other. Many faces sagged in despair.

***

Tears rolled down Ron's cheeks as he sat in his office. Sobs wracked his chest. No man should ever have to make decisions like this. No man should ever have to lead in what was going to follow. He felt a presence–the Prophet.

The Prophet, Mohammed Al Jar, had appeared on Earth as the United World Government was forming. He had an ability to bring people together in their beliefs. Faithism had absorbed the world's faiths, stopping the religious wars that plagued humanity for thousands of years. Ron and Katharine had journeyed through the metaphysical with him. They went beyond the Collective mind, beyond the realms of the Universe.

The Prophet: [Ron, you must remember that no souls are lost. They move on. You are not killing people, just removing them from their suffering. You and Katharine have seen where souls go after death. Do not be tormented. You do not send them to a worse place.]

Katharine: [I know you're focused on those who won't be saved. Don't anguish over the dead, because you know they aren't lost. You must focus on those left here.]

Ron: [The people here must make decisions as to which countries will live and which will die. Many are friends. They will take these deaths into their hearts and some won't survive. Why would the representative from a country destroyed by plagues, starvation, and the rats want to stay? They have no nation to represent.]

The Prophet: [I will take on much of that task, visit them, and alleviate the pain.]

Katharine: [Ron, people will form alliances. The politics of nations is about to fall. Camps and cities will be divided into new nations in miniature, because land is no longer the currency of power. We will move people from some areas into the supported sites. The population will grow, but it will be diverse.]

Ron: [I can see what you say is right. But that pushes the decision of who is to be saved to lower levels.]

Katharine: [Perhaps it should be.]

The Prophet: [I can help with that, too.]

Ron: [How?]

The Prophet: [By showing people that death is not the end of life but the end of struggle.]

Ron: [Will people accept that?]

Katharine: [Ron, we saw that if you limit your perception to your senses in the physical world–sight, taste, smell, touch, and hearing–the physical world becomes your limit. Existence beyond is unimaginable. The Prophet showed us that.]

Ron: [People won't be abandoned passively.]

The Prophet: [Some won't, and nothing will change them, but others will understand. In the end, the result is the same. There will be another massive die-off. The only questions are who and how many. Under the conditions on Earth, society cannot support a billion people. If decisions are not made, civilization will be lost, and many more will die. Humans may become extinct. In a million years another species will arise that has intelligence and creates another civilization. Or maybe it will become the era of Homakuwa.]

Ron's head hung and his shoulders shook. [You just described the end of my species. It is as though Homakuwa has humanity as a pet and must decide to put it out of its misery. I cannot do this.]

The Prophet: [I will meet with the representatives and explain to them what is at stake. They are people of honor and will do what is needed.]

Chapter Five

The five people making up the panel to decide the fate of humanity represented the continents of Europe, Africa, Asia, North America, and South America. Without representatives were Australia and Homakuwa. Australia would be supported with food, but they didn't need troops. The camps and cities were isolated within the interior and not under the same threat as other areas. Homakuwa was under no threat from outside forces.

"Ladies and gentlemen, your unenviable task is to decide how to consolidate our populations so that our remaining resources will ensure survival," said Ron. "I am not a voting member and will only moderate." The faces before him were lined with stress, for they understood what lay ahead.

The wrangling began, and Ron worked to keep them on the path. In the end, the camps and cities chosen were the ones that could best be defended and had the best logistics for supply. Agreements were made on the makeup of the populations of these supported cities by nationality. As Katharine predicted, within the protected areas, nationality took place on a miniature scale.

Military personnel were present to advise in locating the enclaves and fortifying them. They would assist in setting up security. The thought of fenced compounds guarded by automatic weapons and armor to be used against fellow citizens tore at Ron's soul. The human species must survive, he kept telling himself, but the visions of shooting starving people overpowered him at times.

The selection criteria of those inhabiting the new city/states was a brutal combination of practical skills, brains and fertility. Tradespeople to keep things running were at a premium. Everybody had to serve terms in security. People had to understand the cost of their survival. Those unable to do what was necessary were asked to leave. Those who didn't produce were asked to leave.

Chapter 6

Through binoculars, Jeremiah watched the man in the white robe walk through the city. Though the sky was dark, power from the OPS kept the lights burning. People thronged around him as he spoke. The crowds grew as he walked until they filled the streets following him into the Sun Devil Stadium.

From his perch, Jeremiah couldn't see inside, but there had to be enough people to overflow the stadium. A glow pushed back the darkness above. He shivered. The cold had arrived, food supplies were low and no help was coming.

Jeremiah was a fighter. There had been no formal election of him as leader, but the old Motorola factory coworkers sensed he could pull them through.

"Boss, what's goin' on down there?" asked Jacob, his number-two man.

Jeremiah handed Jacob the binoculars.

"Where's that glow comin' from?"

"I don't know, Jacob, but we're not going down there to find out."

"Boss, I think that's Delta goin' into the stadium! Boss, that's my wife! She's goin' in. I gotta stop her."

"You cannot go there. If you do, you will be lost. It's too late," Jeremiah said, holding him down.

Jacob struggled, but Jeremiah's bulk was too great. At last, he lay still, except for an occasional sob.

"I am sorry, Jacob. Delta was a good woman. I worried about her as times got tougher. I…"

"Shut up, Boss." Trembles coursed through them from more than just the cold. "Let's get outta here."

They started along the darkened streets toward the abandoned church now called home. Small and wiry, Jacob scurried ahead, leading the way, but Jeremiah saw the droop of his shoulders.

Phoenix was a refugee city when the Catastrophe hit, and the population had tripled. People swarmed the streets, mobbing the food distribution centers. Lately the crowds had dwindled. What was happening?

At the steps of the church, Jeremiah turned to look at the empty street behind. Where were the people going? He entered the kitchen. A medium height, medium build, medium hair, medium looks woman approached. "Hey, Ruth. At the food distribution center yesterday, was it packed as usual?" Jeremiah asked.

Ruth more than liked Jeremiah. He was handsome, with dark curly hair, penetrating black eyes, and a powerful build. "Nah. There wasn't many, but they wasn't givin' us much food either. It weren't enough for more than a couple of days."

He nodded. Yeah, something was going on. Another thing he noticed–fewer lights in the city. When the refugees first arrived, every building was lit, but not now. Sitting at the table, several cats wrapped around his legs to be stroked. Some of his followers wanted to get rid of the cats, but he liked them. Besides, out in the city, the rat population was increasing. Jeremiah hated rats.

Jacob joined him as Ruth put plates of beans and rice on the table. The meals were barely adequate. Although Ruth was a good cook, she didn't have a lot to work with.

"Jacob, tomorrow send out a crew and start scavenging from the stores. Get everything that is edible–canned goods, dried food, concentrates, all of it. At the pharmacies get vitamins, medical supplies bandages, hydrogen peroxide, alcohol, anything else you find. I want all of it."

"Boss, they already supply us with all that stuff."

"Yeah, but for how long? I have been having strange dreams lately. I see the city empty. The air reeks of death and rats run the streets–only the rats. I think that man in the robe has something to do with what's happening. We had better find weapons, too. We are going to have to fight to survive."

***

Symptomatic of cities around the world, Phoenix was hit by a series of disasters, devastating the population. First, an H1N8 influenza plague quickly overwhelmed medical facilities. With the dead piled in the streets, next came the rats and bubonic plague. Pyres raged throughout the city as bodies burned to stem the raging epidemic. The UWG stopped supplying food and medical supplies. The distribution centers were abandoned. Within two months, the streets were deserted and the city quiet. A few miraculously escaped the diseases and began scraping out a living.

Civilization broke down as the cities were abandoned. Hundreds of thousands gathered in the large arenas, tributes to the days of huge sporting events, and awaited their end, seeking the comfort of companionship. The Prophet was with them, his aura of peace suffusing into them and leading them from this world of suffering.

Survivors competed with the rats for food and warmth. The cities descended into barbarism. Northern cities were ruins, deserted and decayed under pressure of the ice floes and winds. In abandoned inland cities in the temperate zones, starvation was rampant, and as the stores of food were depleted, the living grew fewer in number.

***

"Jeremiah, we lost another scouting party. Billy and Micha didn't come back from the subs."

Jeremiah's group, like most of the small bands, had no name for themselves. The church they occupied was the fourth building they had moved into as they roamed the ruins of Phoenix. They stayed in one area until everything edible had been stripped and then moved on. Scottsdale was the next target. Jeremiah looked at the man in front of him.

"Aw shit, Jacob! That's the second pair this month. What do we know?"

Jacob was a small, shriveled man. He had quick motions and scurried like a rat. He survived, no matter what it took.

Jacob shrank back from the imposing figure. He hated to give bad news to Jeremiah. When their leader lost patience with bad news, the messenger might be offered for dinner. He looked for the telltale flashing eyes and furrowed brow. Not seeing the signs of anger, he swallowed and began speaking in his high-pitched nasal voice.

"We sent them into the subs section, you know, out in the valley. There are schools we thought might have canned stuff. Nobody's seen nuthin moving there in a month. It looked like the Mexi's left or died out. So yesterday, we thought to do a little scoutin'. They was gonna report back so's we could mount a scavenging party. Only they didn't come back."

Jeremiah pushed a stringy lock of black hair from his face. "It is what I would have done, too." Jacob relaxed a little. "I want you to get three others. Arm up and go see what happened. Report back to me tomorrow. God be with you."

Shit, Jacob thought, walking through the door. I don't wanna go out there tonight. But he dare not defy Jeremiah. The earlier the better. Best to get this over. He pointed at a group. "David, Abbie, and Ruth, let's get to the armory. We got a little walk to take."

"You're kidding!" whined David. "It'll be pitch black in an hour."

"All the more reason to go now. Bring Charlie."

Mutely, the group picked out rifles and pistols. As they left the compound, Charlie, a large black Lab, paced them. An hour later, they reached the edge of the suburb.

"I don't wanna go straight in," said Jacob. "Let's go round east for a mile and come in that way. If they're in there, they won't be looking for anything comin' in from the desert side."

The road of cracked pavement was barely visible in the darkness. Charlie ranged ahead of them. After a half hour, Jacob whistled softly. Charlie returned, and they turned left onto a side street. Again, Charlie scouted ahead. Ten minutes later, Charlie nosed against his leg. Jacob called a halt. There was something. They crept forward.

Charlie whined quietly. Jacob followed his gaze to the right. An office building with the windows broken out lay in the darkness. They were on recon, not search and destroy. Jacob motioned his team back, and they cut between buildings to the left and went down the alley. At the end of the block they moved back to the street. Charlie looked up the street the way they had come and growled. They turned the other way and continued. A half hour later, Charlie again nosed against Jacob's leg.

They inched forward and heard voices. In the darkness, he made out a community center building ahead. The windows were blacked out, but light showed through a crack. Outside the door, a man shifted his feet, scraping the sidewalk. Jacob was tempted to return. He had the information he needed: there were people in this sub. But Jacob wanted more. He whispered in Abbie's ear.

"You stay here. If we're not back in an hour, head home and let Jeremiah know there's people here."

Abbie nodded and hunkered down out of sight between two trash bins. Jacob disappeared into the blackness. A few minutes later, he joined David and Ruth. "Let's look around. Might be a way to see in." The building was circular, and in the back was a trash bin piled almost to the roof with boxes. "David, stay here with Charlie. Throw a rock on the roof if anyone comes–not a boulder either."

Ruth and Jacob were both small, easily scaling the boxes onto the roof. They crept over it, peered from the edge at an internal courtyard. Light from inside spilled out, shining into an empty pool. Two figures were in the pool. One was sitting on the bottom with hands tied behind its back. Ruth grabbed Jacob's arm as Micha moaned. The other figure hung upside-down from the ladder. Its throat gaped and blood had pooled beneath it. Yeah, it was Billy. His mouth was open and from his blood-covered face, blank eyes stared. Chunks of meat had been sliced from his thighs and buttocks leaving bone showing. A woman stirred a large stewpot boiling to one side.

A burst of laughter came from inside, followed by rapid Spanish. They were Mexis. With no chance of getting Micha back, they returned to the pile of boxes. "Did you see anything?" asked David. Jacob just nodded and started back to their church.

***

Jacob shifted from one foot to the other, watching Jeremiah watch him. "The Mexis caught Billy and Micha. They had parts of Billy in the pot, and we had no chance of getting Micha back. Nuthin to do but come back and report." Jacob's voice was even higher than usual with the bad news.

Jeremiah face clouded. "How many were there?"

Jacob rubbed his grizzled jaw. "We couldn't see inside, but outside at least four, assuming the outpost had two people. There's sure another outpost on the main street goin in, probably with three, maybe more. I'd guess two more outposts at the compass points. That's at least fourteen."

"That is half our number. Any guns?" Jeremiah asked.

"Didn't git that close. So what ya wanna do? Go after 'em, or just take one or two when our pot gets empty?"

"First thing we're going to do," said Jeremiah, "is beef up our perimeter security. They know we're here because Billy and Micha told them. I want overlapping posts. Put dogs on the ones facing the Mexis. No surprises." He stared hard at Jacob. "They will be coming."

"Yur right 'bout that," said Jacob.

"We will ignore the Mexis for a while. Send out another scout party. Check for provisions on the other side of the sub the Mexis' are in. Ignore the office buildings, the hospitals, and the grocery stores. They are already empty. The Mexis may not have thought about the schools."

"What you gonna do when the Mexis come?"

"First thing is to capture one and find out how many they are. Then we do some recon to see if any other groups are operating here. We only need one to question. Don't let any others get back to report, understood?" said Jeremiah, looking sternly at Jacob.

"Oh yeah, I unnerstand." Jacob left.

Chapter Six

Jamie Wong: [Kit, I'm ready to show you what we have on that greenhouse idea of yours.] Jamie was in his lab in Ocealla. He pushed a button, and a hologram formed above the table. Though Kit was thousands of miles away, he was able to see through Jamie's eyes.

A white egg floated in the air. [Let's start with this.] The egg stretched and became a white worm. As Kit watched, it grew longer and fatter. There was nothing to give it scale, so he didn't know the size, but it stopped growing, and began to inflate, like a long balloon, but with ribs. When it stopped, Jamie said, [This is our greenhouse.]

A speck appeared beside it. The view expanded until the speck resolved itself into a man. The greenhouse was gigantic!

Jamie: [This organism is a combination of plant and animal. It is able to use the beamed energy from the Orbiting Power System much as a plant uses sunlight to grow. The low light on Earth is not a concern. Once the growth stops, the skin hardens into a membrane that absorbs the microwave energy from the Orbiting Power System and converts it to light for the plants. It continues to live, but in a semi-rigid state. It is capable of repairing and replenishing itself, but it is immobile. The greenhouse lives off microwave energy, water, and micronutrients from the soil. The growth time is three months.]

Kit: [This is amazing. I didn't understand the scale at first, but these greenhouses are huge!]

[The Architect is analyzing the design now. We'll grow the digital model and then a smaller one to ensure no problems. The interior is quite isolated from the environment. The water inside is treated by the greenhouse and recirculated. Make-up water and nutrients must be added as produce is removed. We can set the inside temperature as necessary. Since the energy continuously comes from the orbiting system, the photoperiod can be whatever length of day is best for the plants.]

Kit: [The greenhouse is part of the growing system, isn't it?]

Jamie: [It's designed to take in wastewater from a sewage plant, and make the nutrients and fertilizers needed. It can also be used to discharge purified water for human use. Inside, we will grow our crops volumetrically and thus be able to produce in quantity, like we did at Kihhim. Kit, I'd like to come and set up the prototype as soon as it's ready.]

Kit: [I've worked with Mayor Sanchez, and we have land secured for the first site.]

Jamie: [I'm really looking forward to this trip to Tucson. Call it nostalgia, but that's where we started. It's a very stable region without hurricanes, only rare earthquakes, and in the temperate zone.]

Kit: [There's a small airport in the old town of Marana we can use once we're up and running. Rich and his salvage operation aren't far away in Phoenix for materials as needed.]

Leticia: [I've been listening, and I like Tucson too. It's not so large that we'll have everybody watching us, and I understand that Kihhim still stands. I'd like to visit it, too. Jamie and I can head there this week. I'll get a Traveler to take us from Ocealla to Puerto Peñasco. If we leave tomorrow, we should get into Puerto Peñasco in three days. Kit, do you want to pick us up?]

Kit and Leticia had been married for decades, but work had separated them for long stretches. He quickly agreed. [I can check out a plane to fly to Puerto Peñasco and meet you there.] He was as excited about seeing Leticia as about the new greenhouse program. It had been so long.

Chapter Seven

The small jet flew over the coast. Even with his night vision goggles, there was little to see. Puerto Peñasco had started as a fishing town in the upper Sea of Cortez. After the Catastrophe, it had died.

The beautiful beaches contained the ruins of the high-rise condos poking up from the sand. The Baja Peninsula had protected this area from the tsunamis that had devastated most of the coastal cities around the world. Kit looked down at the ghost town. The plane circled, and he saw the shape of the Traveler nearing the beach. The Travelers were Jamie Wong constructs of whale-like proportions for transporting the humanoid citizens of Homakuwa. For this Traveler, it was a one-way trip. There was not enough food for it to get back to Ocealla. It saddened him.

With the tide out, there was plenty of flat sand for a landing strip. Kit taxied toward Leticia and Jamie as they sloshed through the shallows after emerging from the Traveler. Each pulled a float with their gear. Leticia met him on the beach with a big hug, not wanting to let go.

"Did you see anybody?" asked Leticia.

"It looked deserted," said Kit. "Maybe with the new greenhouse design, this town can thrive again. When the skies clear, it will have plenty of sunlight, and the ocean is an unlimited source of water, providing Jamie can get the greenhouses to desalt seawater."

"I already have," said Jamie. "Peñasco also offers a seaport for transporting produce, and it is warm. We'll talk."

"Do you want to go?" asked Kit.

"We've been underwater in Ocealla for so long," Jamie said. "I don't know about Leticia, but I just want to stand here for a while, maybe walk around. Though we're in twilight, it's a lot brighter than two-hundred feet under water. We never get wind there, you know."

Kit laughed. He hadn't been in Ocealla for a while, and he did miss the peace of it. He looked at Leticia as the wind ruffled her hair. Her eyes were closed as if she were absorbing the whole environment. He was happy to be standing next to her.

***

Their small plane dipped a wing so they could see Marana before continuing into Tucson. They had on night vision glasses, but there was not much to see. The Santa Cruz River had flooded during the rains and washed away many of the structures. It was as Kit had said–lots of flat land. They circled and Kit pointed out the wastewater treatment plant.

Kit: [We're making a lot of progress here, creating a model for others. We're opening up the old pipeline from there to the first site. You can see the excavations into the mountains for the support community for the greenhouses. As the greenhouses expand outward, we'll start other communities. It will facilitate wastewater introduction and cut down on commuting problems.]

Looking down on Tucson, many of the houses showed life, but they were in shabby condition.

Kit: [Refugees moved in. We're forming a plan to do something with them, because our stores of food won't last another year. Rich thinks we can move people into excavations in the mountains. We could have gone underground in the valley, but with increased rainfall, there could be flooding.]

Houses still stood, not because people lived in them, but because of the energy collectors that covered the roofs.

Kit: [We're moving the solar collectors onto structures on the mountains. The houses are deteriorating, but we need energy while we move things. Even though it's August, there's snow on the tops of the mountains surrounding the valley, a testament to how much the Earth has cooled.]

Leticia remembered times before the Catastrophe. August was the rainy season here. Wind currents brought moist air from the Gulf of Mexico, and as it rose over the mountains, thunderstorms dumped rain on the thirsty desert. Now, there was snow in the winter, and rain throughout the summer. It was still a desert, but that was because nothing could grow without light. They were going to change that.

Kit taxied up to the old General Aviation terminal. A well-dressed man met them as they stepped from the plane. He was of average height with a dark complexion, black hair, and a large moustache. He extended a hand. "Bienvenidos a Tucson," he said in a deep rolling voice. They shook hands. It was much cooler here than in Peñasco because of high elevation and being away from the sea. "I'll have your bags taken to the hotel," said the man.

As they entered the building, Leticia introduced herself. "I'm Leticia Gardner, the Vice-President of Homakuwa, and this is Jamie Wong from Ocealla."

"I am Enrico Sanchez, the mayor of Tucson, but call me Rico." They entered an elevator, which took them down to the underground transport-way. "Tell me of your visit. All Kit told me was that some important people would be arriving. Is that you? It must be, because we don't get many planes landing here." His smile betrayed the humor behind the question.

Jamie, Leticia, and Kit laughed. "I don't know how important we are, but we're here," Leticia said. "Kit may have told you that we have some wondrous things to show you, and I hope we'll be working together."

"Ooh! Now you have even more of my interest," said Rico.

They stepped from the elevator and onto the underground transport-way. Leticia remembered these people movers from her time in Washington before the Catastrophe. It was like a conveyor belt but moved at different speeds. The edge toward the sidewalk moved slowly to allow people to step on and off. The opposite side moved much faster. They moved toward the center and were whisked away with the lights of stores and businesses zipping past. As the number of lights increased, Rico moved them to the edge of the transport, and it slowed until they stepped off onto a sidewalk.

"If you wish to freshen up, I can take you to your hotel," Rico said.

"We're fine," said Leticia. Jamie nodded.

"Okay, my office is through here. We can talk, and I'll have refreshments brought in." He guided them down a hallway, opening a glass door with the wording 'Mayor's Office.' As they passed a young woman at a desk, Rico said to her, "Charlene, can you bring water and coffee for our guests?"

The mayor's office was simply furnished. Pictures of the mayor with other politicos, and one with his wife, a short dark woman with a brilliant smile, and a teenage girl with an equally brilliant smile decorated the walls. His desk contained only a monitor. Gesturing for them to sit on a couch, he pulled a chair over for himself. Within minutes, Charlene appeared carrying a tray with cups, a coffee pot, and a pitcher of water, setting them on the coffee table before leaving the room.

Looking at Leticia, Rico said, "Enjoy the coffee. It may be the last we have." His bright smile peeked from beneath his moustache. "You intrigue me. I know very little of Homakuwa, except that it is a nation in the sea. Tell me more."

"The easiest way is to show you a video," Leticia said, as she took a small projector from her pocket and placed it on the coffee table. Pressing a button, an image formed in the air.

A hologram of a pretty woman appeared. Quite tall, she had white skin and shoulder-length blonde hair. Behind her was an underwater view looking out into a swarm of sea life.

"I'm Katharine Levey, president of the nation of Homakuwa, an undersea civilization and the second native intelligent species to inhabit the Earth." Her eyes sparkled as she smiled.

"First, a little history of Homakuwa. We began as a small community in Southern Arizona made up of scientists and engineers." The hologram changed to show a desert valley below a tall rounded granite mountain. Three huge glass pyramids covered one hillside of the valley, and a large cavern penetrated the side of the hill. "This was our home, Kihhim, which is Tohono O'odham for 'the village' or 'the place where I live.' The mountain in the background is Baboquivari Peak, the legendary birthplace of the Tohono O'odham people. We were a self-sufficient community, almost independent from Earth. This idea was embodied in the Biosphere 2 project near Tucson."

The hologram showed a several-story high glass structure nestled in the foothills of the Santa Catalina Mountains. "Biosphere 2 was a scientific experiment to create an enclosed environment where everything was recycled and reused. Inside the four-acre sealed greenhouse, eight Biospherians grew their own food, recycled their waste, and generated their own air for two years. Other than energy and information, nothing passed from outside into the biosphere or from inside out. It was a space colony on Earth. Many of the residents of Kihhim came from the Biosphere 2 project when it ended. They believed humans had to learn how to live within the environment or eventually perish.

"As part of being self-sufficient, we used the genetic ability of our resident scientists to enhance food production in our greenhouses." The view changed to a plant-filled glass structure several stories high. It was one of the glass pyramids. Tiers of growth filled every space.

"In many cases, we modified existing plants for our greenhouses. In other cases, we created new plant species. We also began to apply genetic designs to animals. After several years, we moved from Kihhim to a large sea-going vessel and became an independent nation at sea." The hologram showed a colossal catamaran with an arched building creating the span between the two hulls. Towering sails rose from each deck. "We called it Kahchk Kihhim, 'Sea Village,' in the language of Tohono O'odham.

"Once we became a seafaring nation, we applied our genetic technology to create new designs and integrate ourselves into sea life. We modified dolphins and humans to make aquatic citizens, and we created other sea species to aid in our conversion to the marine world."

The hologram showed dolphins and a man-like creature with webbed hands and feet. "We also created completely new species." The hologram showed a squid-like creature with eyes surrounding its body and hands and fingers at the end of its tentacles. "We think of Homakuwa as a single new species–different from humans, not because of the physical characteristics of our citizens, but our ability to create life to meet our needs. After several years, we changed from a surface marine civilization to an underwater aquatic civilization where we grew our cities and expanded throughout the world." The hologram changed to an undersea view. A silvery layer of bubbles hung suspended. The view moved toward the layer, and it resolved itself into a huge cluster of bubbles filled with human-like creatures. Swimming around the outside were other creatures—some like dolphins, others like squids.

"How interesting," said Rico. "I knew of the legends of Baboquivari Peak because my ancestors are Tohono O'odham, but I didn't know of Kihhim. After seeing the underwater city of Ocealla, I remember stories of you. You are another species?"

"We consider ourselves so," said Leticia. "Jamie, Kit, nor I have had much alteration. I have been working with the United World Government for quite a few years in other countries. Jamie just came from Ocealla."

"Jamie does look pretty pale," said Rico. They laughed. "Okay, why are you here?"

"I am sure you are aware of the impending food shortage. Our stored food is running out, and we cannot grow much in the dark. I did notice you have greenhouses, but we're here to show you a whole new idea in greenhouses and growing food. We want to try it in Tucson before expanding it."

The mayor's eyes lit up. "Tucson!"

"In the introduction to Homakuwa, I said we design life as you design building and tools. Let me show you," said Jamie. He picked up the projector and pushed a button. He set it back on the table. A pale white egg hovered in the air.

"This is how we start. Homakuwa has designed a new species. It begins life as a large egg." The hologram showed a man standing beside a three-foot egg. "Once hatched, it grows rapidly in a long wastewater trough and feeds on waste products." The hologram showed the egg in an earthen ditch. It cracked open, and a white larva-like creature emerged, filling the trough. The major stared intently.

Jamie continued, "Large isn't an adequate description for this organism. The small ones are three-hundred feet long and twenty feet wide. Once the trough is full, it begins to swell, spilling over the edges of the trough until it is sixty feet wide and thirty feet high." The hologram illustrated this growth and reshaping. The mayor's face registered his surprise.

"At this point, food is taken away, and it devours most of its own insides, becoming almost hollow. Nutrient-rich liquid is then fed to it, and its skin becomes translucent. Though still alive, it is inert and ready to be filled with plants." The hologram showed a huge, empty greenhouse.

"The ribs form the structure, and the skin is the cover." Jamie smiled, pointing. "Ducts and tubes remain and circulate liquids throughout. It is a living self-repairing greenhouse and feeds on wastewater and the waste products of the greenhouse growth. The whole process takes three months to complete."

"This is amazing!" exclaimed Rico. "You built this?"

Jamie nodded. "Replicating this throughout the world, most agriculture will be greenhouse grown. Homakuwa also designed plants for greenhouses that are much more productive than surface plants." The hologram showed the inside of the greenhouse filled with plants. "The human population will feed itself on a fraction of the land required in the past."

The mayor's eyes grew wider as he watched "This is magic!" . "This greenhouse uses the energy beamed down to create light directly for the plants?"

"Yes, your honor," said Kit.

"Forget that *your honor caca*. And it treats waste water to make fertilizer?"

"Yes, Rico. It is almost magic."

"What do you need to get started?"

"We need land and a stream of waste water," said Jamie.

"Which is why you and I have been talking about abandoned farmland in Marana," said Kit.

"How soon do you want to start?" asked Rico. He looked at Kit. "We've picked out the plots and started preparing them."

"We'll have the prototype eggs here in three months. What do we need for permitting?"

"Just a moment." The mayor went to his desk and spoke to the monitor. He returned. "I have someone coming here to discuss that."

Within a few minutes, there was a soft rap on the door. Charlene stuck her head in. "Dylan Jackson is here, sir."

"Show him in, por favor."

A short man with receding hair, thick glasses and a wrinkled shirt stepped in. "Sir, you wished to see me?"

"Dylan, this is Leticia Gardner, Jamie Wong, and Kit Carson from the nation of Homakuwa." They shook hands. The mayor continued, "They want to conduct a project in Tucson which they'll explain to you later. I'm assigning you to them. Please take care of any permitting they require and assist them in the logistics for this project. What you will discover is this plan may save many lives, even humanity. This could be the most important undertaking we will ever be involved with."

Dylan looked at the three strangers. "What's Homakuwa?"

"They will explain it all. Dylan, keep me informed as to the progress. Nothing is to slow or stop this project. Give me a list of your other work, and I'll get it reassigned. This will be your only responsibility, and you answer only to them and me. Save your questions until you accompany them to the conference room where you will be shown amazing things. After you've seen what they have, take them to their rooms and come back here. We will have a lot to discuss."

"Rico," said Leticia, "let's keep this confidential until we get things going."

The mayor nodded. "You are exactly correct." He turned to Dylan. "Confidential." His finger was in the air. "That means you don't tell even your wife. She's worse than the daily newspaper." Dylan's head bobbed, and they laughed. "I will see you," he looked at Dylan, "in a little while. If you," he looked at Kit, then Jamie, and finally at Leticia, "need anything, call me. Here's my direct contact number. Don't give this to Dylan's wife either." They laughed again and shook hands. Dylan guided them down the hall to another room.

Jamie: [Once we're supplying Tucson, we can put the greenhouses around any of the other cities. As the glaciers retreat and we're able to move north and south, the program can easily be expanded.]

Chapter Eight

The ceremony to mark the opening of the first living greenhouse was a well-publicized event. The dais and grandstand erected at the Marana site were dwarfed by a fully-grown greenhouse. The giant tube glowed from the conversion of the OPS energy to visible light. Plants crowded the transparent doorway.

The celebrity attendees included United World Government president Ron Carson and mayors from the larger cities. Many attended via holo broadcast. All were sure to be in camera range whenever they could. Both Leticia Gardner and Katharine Levey representing Homakuwa were there, along with Kit Carson and Jamie Wong. Tucson Mayor Enrique Sanchez was delivering a short introduction for Representative Levey. As she took the dais, applause broke out. She smiled acknowledgement and cleared her throat before speaking.

"Behind me is the hope of our race for survival. The dark skies and twilight we live under will last for years and our stored food is running short. Without a new source of nourishment, we will suffer widespread starvation within two years. Our scientists designed this as the first of many solutions." She gestured behind her.

"This greenhouse is a designed living thing. Six months ago, it started growing. Three months ago, we seeded it, and the plants began to grow." She held up a tomato. "This is the first produce from our new food source." She handed it to Mayor Sanchez, who sliced it and passed pieces to some of the people sitting in the front. A cheer arose from the crowd.

"We have more greenhouses growing here. Once we get them established, we'll start producing the larva en masse and distribute them throughout the world." Again, she gestured behind her toward the glowing mass. "This one is growing familiar plants–tomatoes, squash, lettuce, and cucumbers. The next one," she pointed to another two-meter egg to one side, "will grow different species of food plants, faster growing and more productive than the natural ones."

Applause broke out in the crowd. She smiled.

"We owe our thanks to the team working on this." She pointed to the group of scientists and construction people grouped to one side. "We will come through this. We will survive." She raised her hands above her head, and a thunderous applause followed. The afternoon was filled with toasting, congratulations, back slapping, and most importantly, the sampling of fresh produce.

***

The Homakuwa team sat together in Kit's apartment. No one spoke aloud, but they were tied together in the Collective.

Jamie Wong: [They didn't acknowledge Homakuwa's contribution much.]

Katharine: [That was on purpose. I spoke with Ron, and we decided that Homakuwa's presence should diminish. We shared the credit for this demonstration of our technology with human partners. Displays of our differences and advancement could inflame those who are jealous, envious, and feeling inferior. We're going to embark on a program to minimize our presence as Homakuwans and just be Earthlings. Our society is far too fragile to sustain hostilities.]

Leticia: [Then the humanoid Homakuwans will play a more prominent part in human society?]

Katharine: [Our long-term plan is to periodically disappear. We don't want to reveal that we do not age. We're thinking that thirty years in human society, and then away for twenty would be a good schedule.]

Jamie: [We could change our appearance. It's easy enough.]

Leticia: [Good thought. What about our management of the Orbiting Power System?]

Katharine: [Leticia, you will be our spokesperson for that society since you are in charge of it. The story line is that humans or at least human-like beings are running it and cannot return to Earth because they lived there too long. I want humans to forget how alien some of us are. We will not mention the colonization and life elsewhere in the Solar system.]

Kit: [Jamie, how long before the seas start to come back?]

Jamie: [Our algae species are starting to take off, and natural predators such as amoeba are appearing but their reproduction rate cannot keep up with the algae. We should be able to introduce the first designed algae eaters by the end of next year. We will have fish species within three years.]

Kit: [We'll need to figure out what to do when the humans want to return to the sea. We cannot afford to turn control of the oceans back to them.]

Katharine: [Agreed. Kit, when you feel the humans are able to handle the greenhouses, I'd like you to start moving into the human political circles– get well known, become prominent, start looking like a candidate for office.]

Kit: [Whew! I haven't done that since before the Catastrophe.]

Leticia: [You and your father are the most experienced with human politics in Homakuwa. After his term as UWG president, Ron's going to have to disappear, and we're going to need to put someone else in office.]

Katharine: [Leticia, I want you to become more prominent as Kit's wife, but also as the emissary with those operating the Orbiting Power System. This has to be a slow rise.]

Leticia: [What about you? You're well known now.]

Katharine: [After my term, I'm going to retire back to Ocealla to act as president there. Ron has been in the public eye for a good while, and he's going to move back to Ocealla, too. With Kit in Tucson and moving within political circles, we'll widen our influence. Our idea is for him to run for office within five years–either mayor or state legislature. This project has put Tucson on the map, and we need to take advantage.]

Katharine: [Leticia, both you and Kit have been away from Homakuwa long enough to break that tie. What we're saying is that humanity needs our help, but with competition for resources, prejudice will rear its ugly head. We never want to confront humans.]

Chapter Nine

Linked into the Collective, Ron Carson, Rich Lewis, Jamie Wong and Kit Carson were looking at the progress made in the program to save humanity.

Ron:[With the consolidation of the populations and the move to Tucson, we've begun the model for the rest of the world. The community of forty-thousand can be sustained until we get the greenhouses growing.]

A hologram of an egg shape appeared in the air above Jamie Wong. It began to grow as he spoke. [We have integrated the greenhouse and the plants inside into a biologic system. By using the energy beamed from the Orbiting Power System to grow and then absorb and re-emit that energy as light that plants use, we no longer are dependent on sunlight striking the Earth's surface.]

[To add project scope,] said Kit, [the area inside each greenhouse is five acres. At present production, it will take one-thousand greenhouses to feed

Tucson's population. The operation of a five-acre greenhouse takes ten people, so a large portion of the population will be working the greenhouses. We're becoming a high-tech agrarian society. The plan is to grow two-thousand greenhouses. The produce from the additional greenhouses will sustain a population while we expand and build another city.] A hologram view showed greenhouses extending from the Tucson Mountains along the Santa Cruz river valley and up toward the Silverbell Mountains.

Rich: [We are excavating into the Tucson Mountains to build housing for those supporting the greenhouses. The city is moving west and north of its present location and underground. To achieve the massive excavation, we designed and tested a prototype machine at an open-pit mine south of Tucson.] A hologram view showed a schematic of the mile-wide hole hundreds of feet deep. The pit had fifteen benches, steps fifty feet high, from top to bottom. As the camera moved down the pit, a pond appeared in the bottom. In the twilight, a large piece of equipment clanked down the ramp on wide steel tracks. Well below the lip of the pit, it turned toward the rock wall. The two people beside the machine were dwarfed by the size. When the face of the machine was against the rock, a high-pitched whine began. A semi-circular hole formed, and blocks of stone came from the back of the machine.

[As you can see, the cutting head is different from the old rotating style of tunnel boring machines. Rather than grinding the face into small rocks, the perimeter of the cutting face has rings of high frequency bits that cut a groove. Transverse bits do the same, carving the rock into blocks that are conveyed out. The fifteen-foot high tunnel is semi-circular with a flat bottom.]

Jamie: [As the excavator advances, it spreads a bacterial paste on the rock wall.] The view neared the ceiling and a gray plastic-like substance was smeared over the rocks. [The organisms rapidly anchor into the rock and harden into an impervious skin. The bacteria continue to grow into the rock, forming structural arches and a living seal. Once cured, another tunnel can be dug above or adjacent to this one.]

Rich: [This excavator began tunneling into the Tucson Mountains and we're building another to use in the Santa Catalina Mountains for the new Tucson. Smaller excavators cut side channels and hollow out areas for homes, retail outlets, and offices.] A three-dimensional diagram of the city plan appeared showing grids of streets in layers. [The housing units are excavated from these corridors.] The camera toured the unit. [A typical unit consists of a main room, kitchen, bathrooms, and bedrooms that double as work stations. The whole excavation process moves quickly. Utility distribution channels cut into the walls handle water and power and remove waste. To furnish these units, we presently have scavenging teams out in the abandoned areas of Tucson.]

Kit: [Once we have Tucson functioning, we will build another community in the mining pit where we tested the equipment. Our plan is to honeycomb the sides of the pit at each bench, greatly speeding up construction. It will easily provide new homes for refugees. We will call it Esperanza, the name of the original mine and the Spanish word for 'hope.' We'll locate two-thousand greenhouses on the old tailings dam. The additional produce will support the next city." A hologram showed the flat expanse of the tailings dam covered with greenhouses. "The mine has plenty of equipment, stockpiles of fuel and photoelectric panels to power construction. And there is water both underground and in the nearby Santa Cruz River. There are other mining operations in this area, and our intention is to turn each into a city. Greenhouses will support the cities, and the cities will supply the nutrients and care for the greenhouses.]

Chapter Ten

Rich was observing the latest construction in Rattlesnake Hill. He was connected with the Collective mind and giving them an update. [This is the floor plan of the education center. Most of the instruction will take place on the com centers in each home. Hands-on training will be done here. This tunnel, I call it a neighborhood, is typical, accommodating two-hundred homes. They should be ready within four months. Kit's crews have shops manned by hired survivors rebuilding or fabricating. The families moving here are going over the inventory online along with the floor plans for their homes. After Tucson, he's going to go to Phoenix.]

Ron: [That sounds good. We're beginning scavenging operations in other cities, but it is dangerous work. There is plenty to scavenge from the inland cities to help us get the housing programs going. Incidentally, we are encountering hostile survivors left behind when we consolidated.]

Katharine: [I shouldn't wonder. They were abandoned to die.]

Rich: [Tucson was lucky to be able to stop the plagues before the population was wiped out. Still, ninety percent died. We also have the massive mining equipment available. Perhaps we should consider shipping some to scavenging sites.]

Ron: [Good idea. Within two-hundred miles of Tucson are at least eight large mining sites. Let's put that together. Haul trucks, loaders, and bulldozers would help.]

Rich: [Kit says there are refugees in Tucson from Phoenix and California who were robotics engineers and designers. We need to send them to Phoenix to start scavenging components. As soon as we remotely operate the equipment, we will cut down on the risk.]

Ron: [Rich, focus on the explorer robots first. Aerial drones and ground crawlers will help locate the materials we want. We will save a lot of time if we map out the ruins and target our scavenging. It will also help with the emotional damage if the operators are remote from the remains we find. We've learned to stay away from large arenas and auditoriums. They are mass graves.]

Ron: [How is Jamie coming with the greenhouse project?]

Jamie: [I'm here. We've designed many species of nutritious plants that grow at increased rates and we're integrating them with the greenhouse itself. We're working on protein vats now that use the plant waste. We're incubating additional greenhouse eggs now for Esperanza and will expand that for other cities soon. Tucson's wastewater has been easy to tap into, so we can expand the distribution pipelines as we go.]

Kit: [There's another wastewater treatment plant to the west we can use, though we'll need to put people there to start it.]

Rich: [Sewer lines are now being installed from the new habitat to the wastewater plant. We'll be ready as people move from the city. Forty families are living here now helping with the excavation and construction. In addition, they're installing the power panels on the mountain so we'll have that done.]

Ron: [The time to develop the greenhouse technology went as quickly as we could make it, but widespread starvation has decimated other areas when the food stores ran out. We're going to need labor to get things going, and the only way that can happen is if we use mechanical help. We need robots and controllers.]

Rich: [I'll get a team together to go to Phoenix to start scavenging electronics. We need mechanical controllers for the scavenging equipment for other sites around the world.]

Ron: [Turn the Tucson operations over to Kit.]

Rich: [What's the situation in Phoenix?]

Ron: [The city is abandoned. There are a few scattered groups of survivors, but they shouldn't pose any great problems, but take security with you.]

Chapter Eleven

Jeremiah sat quietly. The consolidation had happened, and the UWG had pulled out the last of their teams little more than a year ago and gone south to Tucson. The temperatures in Phoenix continued to drop, but it didn't yet freeze every night. When the UWG left, they emptied their warehouses and took the food with them, but they did not ransack the city. Many people followed the Prophet into the arenas, such as the Sun Devil arena and the Glendale arena. They didn't return.

Inspecting one, Jeremiah had seen thousands and thousands of bodies piled atop each other. A month later, he moved away. The stench made the area impossible. Even the coyotes left. Only the rats stayed. When his small band of followers ran out of food, they returned, not for the bodies–for the rats.

His reverie was interrupted by Jacob's call.

"Boss, boss. Noah's back from a scouting party to the south. The UWG's invading. They got big equipment and plenty of soldiers."

"Did they see him? Do they know we are here?" asked Jeremiah in a worried voice.

"Nah, he was careful."

"Could he tell why they were back?"

"Nope," said Jacob. "He just watched 'em come in on the Interstate with equipment. It was mostly trucks, with a few RV's."

"I think we better have a look," said Jeremiah heaving his six-foot three-inch frame from the chair. "Get David and Abbie. Bring Charlie and guns and a pair of binoculars."

"Sure, boss."

***

They heard the trucks long before they saw them. A column of eight trucks rolled down the old Interstate 10 and exited at the Motorola plant. Jeremiah watched them pull up to a loading dock. Soldiers formed a perimeter, and coverall-clad people opened the roll-up door. They entered and lights came on inside. Nothing happened for an hour, then a beeping noise rang out, and a line of forklifts started filling the trucks. As soon as a truck was full, it left, accompanied by soldiers. Another truck would back up to the dock. On the interstate, headlights showed a line of trucks heading their way.

Jeremiah had worked at this plant before the Catastrophe. He realized they were scavenging electronics. Four hours later, they were still at it and showed no sign of leaving. Parking lot lights were turned on, and they had set up RVs for the workers and soldiers in the factory. This was not a short-term operation. A second shift took over for those inside. There might be an opportunity here, thought Jeremiah.

"Boss, you're thinking again. What are you gonna do? They got food down there, but there's too many soldiers to attack. What's your plan?" Jacob asked.

"I think the Lord sent us an opportunity. Get me a white sheet and a pole."

Jacob gave him a strange look, and then sent Ruth off to an apartment building in the next block. She returned in twenty minutes with a sheet and a closet pole.

"Jacob," said Jeremiah, "I am going down there."

"Boss, you sure? I mean they could shoot you."

"Yes, they could, but I do not think they will. We might be able to work with them for food."

"You mean like a job!" exclaimed Jacob.

"Yes, like a job. It sounds nice, does it not?"

"Yeah, Boss. It does."

"If I do not come back, you are in charge, Jacob. Ruth, did you hear that?"

She nodded.

***

At the sound of the rifle bolts clicking home, Jeremiah had doubts that this was a good idea. A helmeted soldier ordered him to halt. "May I put this flag down? It is a little heavy."

"Yeah, okay," said the soldier, "but keep your hands up. What do you want?"

"I have an offer for the man in charge."

***

Rich Lewis was connected to the Collective mind.

Rich: [Ron, Katharine, Leticia, I want you to hear this. One of the survivors is here.]

"Jeremiah, you're offering to help us scavenge?"

"I used to work here as maintenance superintendent. I know where everything is. If you tell me what you need, I will show you where it is."

"What have you been doing since the UWG pulled out?"

"Trying to stay alive," said Jeremiah, shaking his head. "I am with twenty-six people, and we are on the verge of starvation. We will work for food. My second in command worked with me in this warehouse, so he can move stuff for you. We can pick, sort, package, whatever you want."

"Where do you live?" asked Rich.

"For the moment, we are in a church, two miles from here. We live wherever we have to. If we worked here, we could live in the change rooms."

Leticia: [Security would be easier. Ask him about other plants and warehouses in the city.]

"Jeremiah, if you had a list of the equipment we need, could you help us out in other plants?"

"Yes, we can tap into other warehouse lists and find almost anything. We might be able to help you build whatever you need. Some of my people were machine operators, and this plant manufactured mechanicals and controllers. It is already set up."

Katharine: [It makes more sense to create our factory within this and other plants rather than transport things back to Tucson.]

Ron: [Our dilemma is that we would be opening up satellite camps, requiring support and security. If we're not careful, we will stretch ourselves thin and overtax our reserves.]

Leticia: [True, but it accelerates our program to get greenhouses going and expand the scavenging programs. I'm for it.]

Katharine: [I'm for it, too.]

Ron: [I'm willing to support it, but we must keep watch on our resources.]

Chapter Twelve

The first explorer robots rolled out of the factory four months later. Jeremiah stood beside Rich Lewis watching. "We never could have made this schedule without you," Rich said to Jeremiah.

"You saved our lives by letting us go to work. We were this far," he held up his finger and thumb pressed together, "from starving. By this time, we would be feeding the rats."

"I'm sorry this whole situation ever arose," said Rich.

"No use whining," said Jeremiah, "All we can do is learn and move forward."

"You and your people have more than pulled your weight. Would you like to stay with us and expand?"

Without hesitation, Jeremiah said, "Yes."

"Cities like Phoenix are easy to scavenge. They were pretty much undamaged. The cities to the west in California are another matter. Some were swept away by the tsunamis. In many cases, the ice has moved in. Yet there are materials we need. That's the part for the drones and robots to play."

Jeremiah looked at Rich. "Las Vegas had a large electronic industry. It is closer, and the last I heard was fairly intact. Most of the people left there after the consolidation died off, so that makes it trouble free."

"Our eventual goal is Silicon Valley," said Rich. "We need chips, but much of the valley is under ice. We also need solar cells. Phoenix has lots of houses with power-collecting roofs, so we'll need to start a program scavenging those. We can modify them in our factory."

Jeremiah turned toward distant mountains. "What does it really look like for the world?"

"The prediction is we'll be in twilight for the next ten years. We're developing plants that can live in low light and cold temperatures, so the world ecology will develop faster than with just nature," said Rich. "We also have a radical greenhouse program. Once online, we'll be able to feed our people."

"What about others still in the wild like we were?" asked Jeremiah. "There was a lot of bitterness over the consolidation among those left behind to die. I mean, I understand why it had to happen, but most don't. The churches held a lot of hatred toward the Prophet, because he led people to their death without a fight."

"I will not deny that is exactly what he did. You never met the Prophet, have you?" asked Rich, knowing the answer. Jeremiah shook his head.

"Perhaps you should."

****

Jeremiah sat in his office looking over inventory lists. There was a soft knock at the door. "Come," he said. A white robed figure entered.

"Good morning, Jeremiah."

Jeremiah was stunned. At last he stuttered, "Gggg good morning."

"There's no reason to be afraid. I am not here to harm you," said the Prophet.

An image of Delta, Jacob's wife, entering the stadium flashed in his mind followed by the mountains of corpses in the stadium. He felt calm flow into him like heat from an almost forgotten sunlight. His mind slowed.

"Here, take my hand," said the Prophet as it appeared from the depth of his robe. Jeremiah looked down and grasped the hand. "Look into my face."

Jeremiah looked up. Penetrating blue eyes met his. He fell into them, and the room swirled. Jeremiah closed his eyes. He felt himself rise and soar into blackness. Clouds whipped by, then stars appeared, something he hadn't seen since the Catastrophe. He began to fly through them and the spots of light became streaks as their speed increased. Ahead lay a concentration of stars, swirling in a spiral. The center was the deepest black he had ever seen, and they were racing toward it. He could feel the Prophet's hand grasping his. Words formed in his mind.

"I'm going to show you where I took those who left the Earth. They are not lost. They have shifted to another plane." The Prophet led Jeremiah into the blackness at the center of the stars. All sensation of matter and being disappeared. His mind exploded as brilliance formed around them. It was not light, for they had no eyes: it was not heat, for they had no body, yet the glow filled them. A sensation of peace satiated him. "Reach out with your mind," said the Prophet.

Jeremiah let his mind expand outward. The presence of other minds surrounded him. It was like the swelling of voices in a chorus. It kept rising in volume and tone, carrying him upward. The Prophet pulled him back. "It is time to return."

They were back in his office. "No souls are lost," said the Prophet. "They move to another level. It is the same with you. Do not fear death. It is only the transition. Those who left have moved on. You have a task for those who remain here, and that task will play a key part in the survival of humanity. Do not take this lightly."

Jeremiah looked again at the face of the Prophet, but it was shrouded in the folds of his cassock. Suddenly he was gone. Jeremiah blinked. He was at peace with the past.

There was a knock on the door. It burst open.

"Boss, boss, we got a problem on the floor. Boss, you alright?"

Jeremiah looked up at Jacob. "I… I think so."

"Boss, you don't look so good. Is something wrong?"

"I just had a strange experience. I need to talk to Rich." Jeremiah rose and walked through the door, leaving Jacob with his mouth open.

***

"You've met the Prophet," said Rich as Jeremiah entered. "Have a seat." Rich gestured toward a chair. "What did you think?"

Jeremiah recovered. "I did meet him, and he took me somewhere or somewhen? I'm not sure."

"It was wonderful, wasn't it," said Rich.

"It was that, but now I am… troubled."

"Why?" asked Rich.

"I now understand why those people willingly went into the stadiums. If I had met the Prophet before, I would have too. Rich, what you must understand is that out in the wild, we did whatever it took to stay alive. Some of the things were horrible, but we stayed alive. Now, I would just give up. I have lost something, and it feels like something vital. The drive to stay alive is gone."

Rich was in the Collective mind.

Rich: [Are you getting this?] Several 'yesses' came back.

"Rich, now I would go into the stadium and become rat food. It is as if the fire that was in me is gone. Sure, it is comfortable and soft and nice, but it is not me. I do not know this new person. I could not go back to living in the wild. I would not survive."

"You don't have to. You're out of that now," Rich assured.

"I understand that, but the instinct and drive that kept me alive are gone, and it is that fire that was so vital to me. I am not me anymore," cried Jeremiah, his voice a wail.

Rich: [I need help here. Can this be undone?]

The Prophet: [He cannot unlearn and go back to the state he was before, but we can change his focus. During his time in the wild, he had to pursue survival single-mindedly. It gave him drive. What we can do is rekindle that drive but widen it to survival of the human race.]

Rich: [I don't think he'll agree to see you again.]

The Prophet: [He will not, but it isn't necessary. I will do what I can, but you need to talk to him.]

Rich looked at Jeremiah. He began to repeat what the Prophet said. "Jeremiah, the fire you had before resulted from your total focus on staying alive. We, and now you, are part of a new focus, and that is to keep the human race alive. If we don't get our greenhouses producing before our stores of food run out, the population will drop below a sustainable level." Internally, Rich was pleading for him to understand.

"Society is a pyramid. At the base are those who produce the basic needs of life: food, water, and housing. As we move up the pyramid are suppliers of security, clothing, and transportation. At the top are the organizers and administrators, the leaders.

Our problem is that our reduced population cannot sustain the level of society we had before."

Jeremiah nodded. Rich hurried on.

"It is technology that will pull us out and push us upward. We must replace the base levels of the pyramid with machines, mechanicals, and you are critical to that work. You need to survive to help them survive. Before, your survival expanded from just you to your followers, who depended on you for survival." Jeremiah looked at him "Now we all depend on you. The fire you think you lost must rekindle and expand from you to all of us."

Jeremiah stared. "But with such a great next life, why bother with this one?"

The Prophet's answer formed in Rich's mind. He spoke, "Without this life, the lessons needed for the next will not be learned."

Chapter Thirteen

Ron: [Rich, how's the Mech manufacture going?]

Rich: [Jeremiah has proven to be a real help. He's taken over the management and operations. He's pretty much on autopilot.]

Ron: [I'm glad to hear that. The success of the greenhouse program means we must accelerate the manufacture of Mechs to operate the greenhouses. I'll need to pull you from there and put you in charge of integrating the Mechs into the greenhouse operation.]

Rich: [Perhaps that's a good thing. I'm sensing resentment toward the UWG and Homakuwa from the locals.]

Ron: [Explain.]

Rich: [The locals are the Wild-ones that were left behind and survived when we had to consolidate. Those who have joined us call themselves the Outsiders. They were thankful for the rescue when we arrived, but underneath is resentment that we left them to die. Our continued presence here is an irritant.]

Ron: [You think we should leave?]

Rich: [Part of the resentment is that they cannot live without our supplies. The scavenging life was going to end–they had gotten everything we left. Ron, these are ex-cannibals. They had nothing to eat but each other.]

Ron: [What should we do? Humanity needs their Mech production.]

Katharine: [I've been listening and I have a suggestion. What if we gave them the means to be independent? What if we gave them greenhouses so they could grow their own food?]

Rich: [If we did that, they could become a manufacturing society. I like it.]

Ron: [You need to realize you are creating a new society that could be in competition with the UWG. There could be conflict in the future.]

Rich: [There will be conflict if we do nothing, and we will lose the mechanical base we need to get society back.]

Leticia: [I've been in on this discussion, too. If we look at each society as an entity, then we are about to create a new one. How it is set up will depend on them. The UWG society is based on the principals of government we had before the Catastrophe. We saw the rise and fall of other societies–monarchy, tribalism, dictatorships, democracy, and communism. They arose because of the conditions at the time they formed. Society evolved.

[For the Wild-ones, they devolved because of the total focus on survival. If we set them up independently, they will find their own society. I don't believe we will be able to set it up for them. Whatever falls out from the creation of this society and the UWG society will be the result of internal conflict, and it may be bloody.]

Ron: [What does that say about the UWG society? Thus far, we've focused on pulling them away from the edge of extinction, but at some point, they will have to actually do something else besides grow food. The Outsiders are a society that scavenges and manufactures to trade to the UWG. The UWG trades food back to the Outsiders. If we give the food production to the Outsiders, what will the UWG have to trade?]

Rich: [We have control of the greenhouses and the power system.]

Katharine: [Are you saying that we use those to control humans?]

Rich: [I'm not sure what else we can do or what the consequences might be.]

Ron: [Let's think this over for a while.]

Rich: [Do you feel I should talk with Jeremiah?]

Katharine: [Let's see what he has to say. He certainly brings the Outsiders' perspective to the table.]

Chapter Fourteen

"Jeremiah, come in. First, you are doing a terrific job. You have become the manager, leaving me with little to do. What do you think of taking over completely?"

Jeremiah stared at him, his mouth open. "I… I would like that." He said at last. "Where are you going?"

"We've got a greenhouse design that works well even in this twilight. I'm going to take over the distribution and erection of those before we starve," answered Rich.

"Where are they going to be operating?" asked Jeremiah.

Oh shit! thought Rich. Christ, he was sharp. Okay here we go.

"We're going to start with the camps and cities. As the ice retreats, we'll expand into those regions," replied Rich.

"You planning on any here?" queried Jeremiah.

"We've talked about it. Some are for it–others are not. What do you think?"

Jeremiah's mind raced as understanding dawned. "You are afraid of us."

"We're afraid that we'll end up with a society of conflict again," answered Rich. "You could easily become strong enough to challenge the UWG."

"Who is the 'We' you keep talking about, if it is not the UWG?" questioned Jeremiah. "It sounds as if there is somebody else involved,"

"I am a citizen of the UWG, but also a citizen of the nation of Homakuwa. Have you ever heard of them?" inquired Rich.

"Before the Catastrophe, I remember something about a nation under the sea. A lot of them were not human, as I recall. They had genetic technology they used to create life."

"You remember correctly. In ways, we were like you. We were despised, feared, hated, and hunted by humans. They saw us as a threat and tried to annihilate us. We survived, and now we are trying to save them." Rich smiled at him and shrugged his shoulders as if to say *Go figure.*

"It's your design of greenhouses, isn't it?"

Rich nodded.

"You control the Orbiting Power System, don't you?"

Rich nodded again.

"You will be trying to bring the Earth back with your genetic designs, won't you?"

Rich just looked at him.

"Why are you trying to save humanity so hard?"

"We've asked ourselves that question, too. No matter how bad they are, humans are our parents. Humans were designed to live in Earth-like conditions. They had dreams of exploring space and the planets, setting up colonies, but the truth is they cannot live outside of their environment. The cost of maintaining that environment elsewhere prohibits its reality in any practical size."

Rich watched Jeremiah turn this over in his head. He continued. "There will be another disaster on Earth. It may well be caused by humans, it may be biological, it may be due to a number of things. The point is the Earth has produced millions of species and millions have gone extinct, as the Earth has changed. No species is permanent," finished Rich.

"You could leave. You already have species in space. Why stay here?" asked Jeremiah.

"Jeremiah, I am human. I have the same characteristics as you. All of us born on or designed for Earth are in this with you. Our cities were damaged and destroyed in the Catastrophe, too. We lost our ecology and our food. If we don't bring the Earth back, we'll perish too."

"You hold the power. Why don't you just take over?" cried Jeremiah.

"Jeremiah, you don't like being controlled, and you've thought of how to throw off that yoke. That's a part of being human. If humans believed we were the masters, we'd be destroyed. We're not that big a nation."

Jeremiah stared at him. "So, we're back to the original question. Are you going to put greenhouses here? Are you going to give a society outside the UWG a chance to survive?"

"Why must you be outside of the UWG?" asked Rich.

"There are many of us who remember that the UWG left us to die. We did unspeakable things to survive, and what you're really afraid of is that we will be stronger than the UWG because we survived. There's a lesson here for you. Conflict and challenge created humans. We cannot survive without that—we will become too weak. Simply put, humans are not made to live in heaven."

Rich looked at him. "What would you do in my shoes?"

Jeremiah sat still, thinking. "To ensure the continued existence of humanity, you need to give us, the Outsiders, and the Wild-ones the chance to grow. Give us the greenhouse technology too. I know you're afraid we would get too strong and enter into conflict with the UWG."

Rich stared. This man was really sharp. He'd grasped the issue immediately.

Jeremiah's gaze was fixed on him. "I will not kid you–that may happen. The decision to consolidate humanity into the camps and cities happened, whether it had to or not. As one with fresh scars from the *benevolence* of the UWG, I understand animosity toward the UWG. You stated the perils of putting all your eggs in one basket, and that is what you are doing with the UWG. Regardless of what you wish, it is in the basic heredity of humans to compete and win. The dominant species will survive."

"What do you see that meaning to Homakuwa and my species?"

"As to Homakuwa being a part of the UWG, you have to, but Homakuwa needs to become invisible. You are different. You will never be a part of humanity. If times get tough, they will attack you. Your wish to keep humanity alive is like keeping a tiger as a pet. At some point, the basic nature will come out, and you'll get bitten, or worse."

Rich stared at him. The Collective had been in on this whole discussion, and Homakuwa would review it. If it showed anything, it was that even Homakuwa didn't completely understand humanity. "You're pretty cynical about your own race."

"I have reason to be," answered Jeremiah.

The Collective was abuzz. "We'll be back to you about the greenhouses, but in the meantime, the manager job is yours."

***

Ron: [I'm impressed with him. My main concern is the bitterness he has toward the UWG.]

Katharine: [Rich, can he overcome that?]

Rich: [When the realities of being in charge of a new society sink in, he will. My concern is some of those under him are not so wise.]

Leticia: [He was right about Homakuwa becoming invisible and in agreement with our own conclusions. We need to continue with our humanoid people in positions of power within the UWG to direct it. We need to do that with the Outsider society too. The only visible Homakuwans will be those operating the Orbiting Power System. As far as Earth knows, Homakuwa has moved into space. We're already partially there. Nobody alive today remembers that the present president of the UWG, Ron, left the surface world decades ago to join Homakuwa.]

Kit: [You want to influence things from behind the scenes?]

Leticia: [We must. Jeremiah is right about the basic nature of humans.]

Jamie: [With the introduction of the greenhouses, the major challenge to survival will be overcome. The rise of a competing society will lead to conflict, but that seems to be what will ensure their survival.]

Leticia: [With our influence, we must keep that conflict from escalating into a self-destructive one.]

Jamie: [We'll need to set up labs on the surface to take over the genetic development projects, and that includes rebuilding the ecosystem of Earth. We can staff them with Homakuwans, but we need humans there, too.]

Leticia: [Tricky to do.]

Jamie: [We'll keep the Architect at Ocealla, though.]

Katharine: [This is a bit of an eye-opening shift from our plan before, but it has a more solid base.]

Chapter Fifteen

The meeting of the Collective was one of the most encompassing they had ever had. It was that important.

Katharine: [We have to consider that Homakuwa will have to disappear from the surface world, and maybe from the Earth.] A stir rolled through the Collective. [The humans are what they are, and I now realize that we cannot pull them along the path of advancement. They are the product of their evolution. Our presence is an irritant because they struggle to survive and we grow beyond Earth. Their species must have conflict to survive, and if we are the source of that conflict, we will either have to fight them or be destroyed.]

Ron and Kit, as the last humans to become Homakuwans, started to object.

Ron: [Katharine, they can change. Look how far they have come from the days of Kihhim.]

Leticia: [Ron, we've made this into a world without the need for conflict, and despite increased food production, we're seeing a decline in their population. They need that goad, or they have no reason to exist. I fear for them. They are my mother and father, for they gave rise to us, but we cannot create a life for them without struggle. It is not in their nature to live in Eden.]

Kit: [What do you propose?]

Katharine: [We should gradually turn over control of the surface world to them. We will support the United World Government and maintain a presence, but as humans. Maybe three or four integrate with them and guide their leaders to minimize the chance they will destroy themselves. A shift would take place over years.]

Ron: [Do we just let them battle each other, kill each other?]

Katharine: [Ron, I don't know. I honestly think they will do that with or without us being here. If we're here, we will be embroiled in their conflict.]

Kit: [What about the Orbiting Power System? We maintain and operate that.]

Leticia: [We will continue to run it and supply power. It's our visible presence here on Earth that will fade.]

Kit: [What about the fishing industry? We manage that to the benefit of us all.]

Katharine: [That will be one area where we maintain a presence but as humans.]

PART 2

Chapter Sixteen

Facing the auditorium filled with UWG delegates, Ron said, "Ladies and gentleman, our greenhouse program is moving forward rapidly. Increasingly large portions of our populations are working in the greenhouses and other labor-intensive tasks. The standard of living in our society on the Earth will depend greatly on mechanicals. We have the opportunity to use them, because we are starting with adequate resources–materials, power, and the computer ability to build them into the base for our society. We can create mechanicals with levels of ability to take over more of the work humans have done in the past. It is those levels of capability that will become a concern. Do we build mechanicals that require human control to operate, or do we give them decision making ability and independent thought?"

Ron could see the idea rolling through the audience, heads nodding or shaking. "One option is to build an Artificial Intelligence, an AI, to control the mechanicals. This would be a computer-based system with the ability to learn and think independently. The AI would reside within a few master systems that control those under them. On the surface, this might appear a simple matter, but there is a moral issue. What would be the status of the Artificial Intelligences, and at what point do they achieve social rank within society?"

A wave of whispers ran through the audience. Ron took a breath and continued. "In a tier-like society, a central AI control system would be built to control lower systems acting as area supervisors. That is a very powerful system. At some level of self-awareness, it could be argued that AIs are another species on Earth. How to treat AI systems is an ethical question we need to discuss. It's better to do so now rather than later. I invite discussion." The hall erupted. As Ron expected, the discussions went late into the night. The humans recognized the problem.

***

Jeremiah walked the floor of the Mech factory, his second in command beside him. "Jacob, are we stocked on chips?"

Jacob had to shout for his nasally voice to be heard over the racket. "Boss, we got about four months' supply and that's it. We're scourin' the city now, but this is the third time, so I'm not holdin' out much hope. Anything from the UWG on those?"

"I sent the request but haven't heard back. We may have to mount an expedition," Jeremiah said.

"Where, Boss?"

"Probably Las Vegas. There was a UWG camp there but they moved to Boulder to be near water. We could go through there to Vegas or take the long way around. Either way, there is a lot of empty desert between here and there," mused Jeremiah aloud.

Piping up, Jacob addressed the problem, "There's a lot of desert every direction. At least we'd be travelin' in twilight 'stead of darkness."

"I'm going to get hold of Rich."

"There's somethin' else, Boss. One of the search crews ranged down to Casa Grande and found more Wild-ones. There's only eight, and they're in bad shape. What ya wanna do with em?" Jacob's eyebrows rose.

"Where are they now?" asked Jeremiah.

"We brought 'em back, fed 'em some and stashed 'em in that ole church we usta live in."

"Guard them. We'll figure something out."

Jeremiah picked up the phone and punched in the number Rich had given him.

Chapter Seventeen

"Jacob, where are you?" asked Jeremiah into the phone.

"Kingman last night; headin' into Searchlight this mornin'. We should be in Vegas tonight. Rich's survey maps showed factories to scavenge," Jacob answered.

"What does it look like north?" asked Jeremiah.

"It's still too dark to see far, but I 'spect that when we see the mountains there'll be snow."

"How's the caravan doing?"

"Those boys operatin' the power system are good. When we pulled into Kingman, the lights started comin' on. Power at the main station was good, an' we had full charges this morning. It should get us to Vegas," said Jacob.

"See much along the way?" inquired Jeremiah.

Jacob understood what he was asking. "Nothin' stirrin.' There's some scavengin' to do, but we'll do that on the way back."

"If there's as much as the survey maps show, you might stay for a while. We will send another caravan with supplies. You can load it to bring back materials." Jeremiah said.

"If there's enough here, I can man up the team for a while. I'll give you a better report as we get closer. Gotta go now, we're nearing Searchlight, an' I wanna scope it out. Talk to ya later, Boss."

Uneasy, Jeremiah knew a lot was riding on this venture. If Jacob pulled this off, they would set up satellite scavenge *and* manufacturing. So far, the land was empty, but who knew what they would encounter in Nevada. From there, they hoped to move west into California, but it was a long drive. The infrared satellite views provided by Rich showed a lot of damage from earthquakes, but California buildings were more resistant, so at least it wasn't flattened. What they did not show was any sign of life.

With no source of manpower, productivity would be limited. He brought that up with Rich, and the UWG was recruiting equipment operators now. The first class of recruits was due in Phoenix next week to begin training.

Additionally, Jeremiah had asked for computer technicians and engineers to begin designing more sophisticated controllers for the equipment. A knock on the door interrupted his thoughts.

"Jeremiah, it's me, Ruth. Uh, we got a problem. The Wild-ones we were watching at the old church escaped. I thought we'd get 'em back pretty fast, so I didn't trouble you about it, but…"

"What happened?"

"They tried to break into one of the food places, and when David went to stop 'em, they killed him. Drug off his body, too. 'Fraid I know what they did then. You wanna put together some people to hunt 'em down?" Ruth asked.

Oh shit! It had happened. "Let me think about it for a while. I'll get back to you." *If Jeremiah had them hunted down and killed (any team he put together would do that and perhaps more regardless of his instructions) what would that say about him? He was a Wild-one once. Yet he couldn't let them go on. Now who had the pet tiger?*

***

Leticia: [We need to put someone with Jeremiah. I don't trust him yet. We're also going to need somebody with Jacob. Something about him does not elicit my trust at all. Any suggestions?]

Rich: [How about Dayton King? He's been running Retseana along with Carol Goldman since the Catastrophe. That city could use a change, as could they. We could send him in with the trainees going to Nevada in a few weeks.]

Leticia: [Okay, that's good for Jacob. What about Jeremiah?]

Rich: [Let's send Carol Goldman to work with Jeremiah.]

Dayton: [Neither of us is very technical. Thought I should point that out.]

Leticia: [You're not, but the Collective is. We can help.]

***

Rich called Jeremiah with the status of the trainees. "Jeremiah, the UWG has the first team of people to send your way for training. I also asked them to send someone to give you administrative help. You can't wear all hats forever."

"Thanks," said Jeremiah. "This has grown into quite an operation. I could use the help."

"You're welcome," said Rich.

"I have another problem to discuss, Rich." There was silence. Jeremiah went ahead. "You remember that comment I made about having a pet tiger, referring to Homakuwa and the UWG?"

Rich answered. "Sure, and I thought it was a good analogy."

"Well, I have one of those now. We are encountering pockets of Wild-ones. We brought one group back to Phoenix, but they escaped and now roam the ruins. They are raiding our stocks. They killed one of our people. I am sure he was eaten. Two years ago, I would have had no hesitation taking care of the problem. Now, I am not sure what to do."

"Hmmm," Rich said as others of Homakuwa joined in. "Humans haven't been too good with irritating groups in the past. The usual response is to round them up and put them on reservations. They either eventually are absorbed or die off. The Apaches of the American Southwest are a prime example of that. They were a society of raiders taking from the agrarian tribes."

"Rich," started Jeremiah, "a reservation is a drag on us, and we are not that solvent yet. My people have no qualms disposing of them. They will wonder if I have gone soft if I do not." For a second he hesitated before adding, "Maybe I have."

Leticia: [It is interesting that he has changed. Was it the contact with the Prophet?]

Katharine: [I'm encouraged by this. Is it time to consider bringing him into the Homakuwa fold?]

Leticia: [We haven't done that in decades. What's to gain?]

Katharine: [Like Rich, I'm beginning to believe that we need him as a leader of the Outsider society, those living outside cities and camps.]

Leticia: [I see where we are going with this. As a society outside of the UWG, they could at least have representation with the UWG. That makes more sense. There are a couple of questions, though. Would Jeremiah join Homakuwa? Would his society join the UWG?]

Rich: [We won't know until we ask. Posing the question could be delicate.]

***

Rich shook hands with Jeremiah. "It's good to see you again. You've done very well here."

"It is good to see you too, Rich. The greenhouse business seems to be good for you. How come you look no older?"

Rich laughed. "Good genes," he joked. He looked at Jeremiah. Here goes. "Jeremiah, do you remember when I told you about Homakuwa?" He nodded. "Would you like to learn more, actually visit Ocealla?"

"To what purpose?" asked Jeremiah.

Leticia: [He's sharp and wary. I like this guy more and more.]

"We want you to consider joining Homakuwa," Rich said.

"Same question," said Jeremiah.

"We can help with issues such as the thorny one you're facing. Also, we're in the 'Save humanity' mode."

"What do you want in return?"

"Homakuwans are loyal. A closeness you can't yet understand bonds us together. We are the descendants of humans. The evolutionary track humans follow that resulted in their being the dominant species on Earth is not the same for us. We don't possess that same drive to dominate the environment," said Rich.

Jeremiah stared at him. "You say that, but you manipulate humanity from the background. Is that not dominance?"

"You are right. It's what we do," said Rich, "but the motive is different. We're doing that to ensure human survival. We don't need to dominate the Earth because we are inhabitants of the Solar system."

Jeremiah's mouth fell open. "There are Homakuwans on other planets?"

Rich nodded. "We also have ships heading toward the stars." Rich saw the oldest dream of humans rekindle in Jeremiah's eyes.

"Can I visit without joining?" he asked.

Leticia: [We've never allowed that without assurance that the person will join.]

Ron: [You did with me. I saw Kahchk Kihhim, and I understood what you were. I understood the potential threat you posed to humanity. You also took me to Ocealla.] He had never asked what would happen if he had chosen not to join.

Katharine: [Ron, you understood it wasn't in our nature to destroy humanity. We weren't competition to you, even though humanity felt we were. Actions we took were purely in self-defense.]

Ron: [That understanding came after I visited Ocealla and joined Homakuwa. 'Self-defense' has been the phrase used to justify wars throughout history, but I know what you are saying. It wasn't the case for Homakuwa.]

Leticia: [Ron, you did try to destroy us.]

Ron: [I did, but after I experienced the Collective, I understood.]

Leticia: [Rich, Jeremiah brings a perspective to Homakuwa that we need. It's fresh and new. It's down to your judgment of Jeremiah.]

Rich crossed his arms and looked down in thought. "Yes, we'll arrange a trip to Ocealla. We could take you on a virtual trip, but I don't believe that would convince you of who and what we are. How soon can you arrange to be gone for a few days?"

"I will get Ruth to fill in while I am gone. If she gets in trouble, Jacob can get here from Nevada in a day. When do you want to leave?"

"Call me when you're ready," Rich said. "We'll get a plane from Tucson within a day."

Chapter Eighteen

Jacob looked at Jeremiah from the monitor. "Boss, where're you goin'?"

"I am going with Rich Lewis. Remember him?" responded Jeremiah.

"Yeah, fine, but where's he takin ya?" persisted Jacob.

"To tour some cities so we can learn more about where our Mechs are going and what they are doing," said Jeremiah.

"Yeah, I'd like to know more 'bout the cities too. We been separate so long, we don't know what they doin'."

"Jacob, Ruth is in charge here, but I want you to talk to her every day. There should be no problems, but help her out."

"Sure, Boss. No problem."

"One other thing, Jacob. We have Wild-ones here causing trouble. I understand you have had problems there, too, which we will handle when I get back. Do not do anything to them for now," Jeremiah admonished.

"We was just gonna send out a huntin' party."

"Wait until I get back," said Jeremiah.

"Yeah, okay. But if we lose anybody, it'll be hard to hold the crews back."

"Yeah," said Jeremiah. "We have the same problem here. Just increase the patrols to deter them."

***

The drive to Tucson lasted four hours. Jeremiah remembered when it was less than two on Interstate 10, but the roads had deteriorated. Neither the cities nor the Outsider communities did road repair outside of community limits. When they bumped past the old town of Marana, Jeremiah saw the glow of greenhouses marching west to the Silverbell Mountains.

"How many greenhouses are there?" he asked, gesturing out the window.

"Almost three-hundred," said Rich, "but only forty are operating. Eventually, we'll have two-thousand. It takes a thousand to feed Tucson, and we'll be exporting food from the others. Without the Mechs, it'll take twenty-thousand people to operate the greenhouses, and three to four thousand more to process and ship. That'll be almost the whole population of Tucson. Here is where most of the Mechs are working and will be for a long time."

Rich exited the highway, passing a mountain on the left. Glowing lights revealed tunnels bored into the mountain. "This is the support community for the greenhouses. The entire town is inside. There are homes, shops, workshops, everything needed. The photo-cells for collecting the energy are on top and up the sides of the hill."

Greenhouses were on either side of the road until a glowing series of buildings appeared on the right. "This is the local airport. Normally we use the Tucson airport, but sometimes this is more convenient." They pulled in and parked–the sole vehicle visible. Entering the control tower, Rich waved at a sandy haired man.

"Jeremiah, I'd like to introduce you to Albert Jackson. Albert is our pilot."

"G'day, mate. Pleased to meet ya."

Jeremiah was momentarily taken aback by the Australian accent. He had not heard it in a long time. "Pleased to meet you, too. You are Australian?"

"Long time ago, mate. I've been with Homakuwa almost since the beginning and lived in Ocealla for ages. Let's board, because I'm told high winds are coming this way. I'd like to be above 'em," said Albert, gesturing toward the door.

The plane was a six-passenger jet. They were the only passengers and sat with the aisle between them. Albert closed the door and entered the cockpit. The engines spun up, and with a hushed roar the plane moved. At the end of the runway, the roar increased, and the acceleration pushed them into the seats.

Jeremiah looked out the window. The glowing cylinders of the greenhouses stretched away until reaching blackness. The plane bucked, climbing through turbulence before it leveled and the ride smoothed.

Rich leaned toward him. "I'm pooped, so I'm going to take a nap. You might as well relax, too. We've got six hours before we get to Hawaii." Jeremiah watched as Rich's seat leaned back and formed around him.

A nap was a luxury Jeremiah hadn't enjoyed in a long time. He searched for a lever to change the seat, but it had already started to recline, shifting and conforming to his body. He yawned and closed his eyes.

***

Jeremiah awoke as the plane banked over the island of Maui to begin final approach. Staring into blackness, Rich's voice startled him. "Maui, like most of Hawaii, is almost deserted. The tsunamis from the meteorite strikes of the Catastrophe washed away most evidence of civilization. All five volcanos in Hawaii erupted, completing the eradication of most of humanity."

"Homakuwa had to clear the runway in Maui when we moved Ocealla north into the temperate zone."

Jeremiah looked out again. In the twilight that was Earth's day, he saw the deserted air strip, with rubble pushed to the sides and a photovoltaic collector. He turned to Rich. "The empty cities are eerie, monuments to humanity, but this is different, a pristine blank slate. I can easily imagine sunlight falling on the immaculate beaches and glints from the water."

"With a big enough eraser, nature can restart quickly," said Rich, looking over his shoulder.

The intercom sounded a tone. "Welcome to Maui." Albert's Australian twang again brought up memories. The landing was so smooth as to almost go unnoticed.

A hand on his arm startled Jeremiah. "Our ride is here," said Rich, directing him to an old style electric car. Jeremiah got in. Soundlessly, the car accelerated.

The barren landscape rolled by, but he saw palm-covered plains reaching to the water. The car slowed as a short beach appeared. "We'll ride on the Traveler from here," said Rich, opening the door. Jeremiah followed him onto the sand.

Rich walked to the water's edge and turned to face Jeremiah. "This is a traveler." He gestured behind with one hand. Half out of the water was a huge fish. It was the size of a whale. While Jeremiah watched, the front opened. "This way, please," said Rich as he walked into the fish. He held out his hand to steady Jeremiah's step. "Have a seat." Lounge chair depressions had formed in the back. Rich sat.

Jeremiah hesitated–sitting would make him vulnerable. "You'll have to sit before we can leave. The initial motion will knock you over," said Rich. Gingerly, Jeremiah eased into the seat which conformed to him. The fish wriggled its way off the sand, and a clear bubble formed around them.

Holding his breath as the water blotted out the gray sky, Jeremiah noticed the motion of the fish become long smooth strokes. At last finding his voice, he exclaimed, "I do not remember any fish like this."

"This is a creation of Jamie Wong. We've had a hard time keeping them alive. Their food supply became rare, but we needed transportation to Ocealla."

Jeremiah silently looked at the dark sea swishing by, his mind absorbing.

Rich interrupted, "This used to be a much more interesting view. Now there's little life. If you put this collar on, it will connect you with the senses of the Traveler. They are much more attuned to the sea."

Jeremiah held the offered collar which appeared to be a neck pillow, though heavier. Once on, he felt a tingle. Instantly, his view extended outward as if the sun were shining again. A few creatures swam around them. He gasped.

"This is amazing," he whispered. More shapes appeared. Some had many tentacles. Others were similar to dolphins.

"It's just the beginning," said Rich. "Close your eyes now, let your mind go blank." Jeremiah complied. With his eyes closed, the view of the sea grew even brighter and clearer. "Now you're seeing through the eyes of the Traveler, without your own senses interfering."

Jeremiah stuttered. "Y… You can interface with animals?" A voice grew in his mind.

Rich: [We do so with each other, too.]

Jeremiah's mind froze.

Rich: [We can't read minds. We can project to you, or see what you choose to show us. Try it. Say in your mind what you want.]

Jeremiah: [You keep saying 'we.' Who else is here?]

Rich: [You and I are focused with each other. No one else is in our conversation unless you want them to be. I'll show you.] A pathway opened and invited Jeremiah to enter. Through Rich's eyes, he saw himself sitting with the collar around his neck. [Look inside me, Jeremiah.]

Jeremiah saw Rich's memories.

Jeremiah: [Why have you brought me here?]

Rich: [Because I believe you can aid us to help humanity.]

Unbelievably, Jeremiah could understand the doubts and fears Rich harbored, along with his hope and vision of a repaired Earth. Now he understood the truth of Rich's answer. Incredibly, he saw himself guiding the Outland community and merging with the United World Government.

Jeremiah: [I do not know if I agree with your vision for me, but your vision of Earth is what I want too, Count me in.] Pulling himself back, he looked outward through his own eyes again. In the distance a layer of bubbles appeared.

Rich: [Welcome to Ocealla. If you reach out with your mind, you can watch us dock.] Jeremiah tried to reach out, but nothing came. [You're working too hard. Just relax. It'll happen.] He did. A view looking at the sea from another perspective formed. In the distance was the huge fish. Other creatures swam around it. It slowed as they neared, until its nose touched the window. The window dissolved, and he saw himself sitting, eyes closed. He opened his eyes and instantly was within himself.

Leticia: [Are you comfortable?]

Jeremiah thought. [I am. You are Leticia Gardner.]

Leticia: [I am. Ocealla welcomes you, Jeremiah.] He rose and stepped into the room. Rich entered behind him. [Good to see you again, Rich. You're looking well. Is surface life agreeing with you?]

Rich: [Great to see you, Leticia. The surface world is fine, but it's always good to come back here. The peace and community of Ocealla is home.]

Leticia: [Jeremiah, are you tired, do you need to freshen up?]

Jeremiah: [I could use a restroom.]

Rich walked toward a wall. [Follow me.] An opening formed into a door. They walked through. Rich pointed toward one side. [Just think of a stall.] One formed around Rich.

Jeremiah thought of a stall, and the floor extruded a wall around him. A toilet seat formed. He used it. He finished and thought of the room again. The stall disappeared, and a sink appeared in the wall.

Rich: [You catch on pretty quick.]

Jeremiah: [Just because I do it does not diminish the wonder of it.]

Rich: [While wearing the collar, you can communicate with the city. The bubble structure is a living being. In fact, Ocealla is a living entity made up of all of us. We link with it, and as a part of it, keep it going. I'll show you.]

They walked through the opening in the wall into another room. Four people were reclined on lounge chairs. In the center of the room was a raised wall with a small pond in the center.

Rich: [Have a seat.] One formed behind him. [Open up your mind and allow it to merge with the room.]

Jeremiah did, and suddenly he was a part of the group. He watched as one person created an opening for another Traveler. A different person regulated a layer of algae at the sea surface so that oxygen flowed down into Ocealla, while carbon dioxide rose to feed the algae. He entered another mind and saw himself sitting in the room.

Jeremiah realized he was looking at himself from the pond. Words formed in his mind.

Blue Streak: [I am Blue streak, a Dahlfin.]

In Jeremiah's mind an image of a dolphin appeared. In a sequence of scenes, it grew a larger brain and changed.

Blue Streak: [I am a modified dolphin. Jamie Wong changed us to become citizens of Homakuwa. There are many of us.] Another image formed. This one was of a man-like creature with webbed hands and feet.

Sean: [I am Sean Steele, and I am an Altered. Jamie Wong modified me from a human so I could become a creature of the sea when I joined Homakuwa.]

Another image formed of a squid-like creature with many arms and eyes. Some of the arms had hands on the ends.

Unweil: [I am Unweil, a Construct. Jamie used ideas from many animals when he created my species. I am truly a creature of the ocean. If you let your mind merge with mine, you can experience the sea as I do.]

Jeremiah allowed his mind to flow into Unweil. New dimensions of senses opened up as sight, smell, micro-electrical pulses, and sound opened a vision of 360 degrees. His head swirled as he was overloaded.

Unweil: [I am sorry. Let me limit the vision.]

Jeremiah's senses became an enhanced view of the sea around him. He steadied himself.

Jeremiah: [Thank you.] He was aware of everything for miles around, despite the darkness of the sea.

Rich: [Jeremiah, I'd like to introduce you to Chetnaz.]

Jeremiah's view changed, and he was hanging in space looking down on the cloud-shrouded Earth.

Chetnaz: [Greetings, Earthling. That's a little spaceman humor. Welcome to Homakuwa, Jeremiah. I'm part of Tashogith Kihhim, the group operating the Orbiting Power System. If you look closely, you can see that the cloud cover over the Earth is thinning here and there, but there won't be sunlight for a few years yet. Jamie Wong built me for life in space. Here's an image of me.]

A creature like a jellyfish appeared. It had eyes in many places around the bag-like body. Many of the arms had hands on the ends, while some arms had eyes on the ends.

Chetnaz: [Here in space, I don't need skeleton or strong muscles. I pull myself along or inflate and jet around. Since I can equalize internal pressure to the atmosphere, I can do well at very low atmospheric pressure. That reduces my oxygen requirement. Without bones, I'm not as subject to radiation damage either.]

Rich: [Jeremiah, what we do is construct ourselves to our environment, rather than change the environment to accommodate us. This means we are not in competition for resources, and we're a passive species.]

Leticia: [On Earth, we're trying to restart the ecosystem by designing life to the conditions that exist now, rather than wait for the generational changes that nature uses. We're starting with the most basic forms of life, algae.]

Jamie: [Jeremiah, little sunlight is reaching the surface of the Earth, but our microwave energy can penetrate. We've designed species of algae that can use that frequency of energy. Once that begins, we can add other species that depend on algae. We're doing the same with other plants.]

Rich: [You've seen our greenhouses. They are grown, not built, and that life-form is a combination of animal and plant. They absorb microwave frequencies on the outside and re-emit it inside as visible frequencies that normal plants use. That allows us to grow food. We have engineered the plants to produce more edible food than they normally produce. The waste products are consumed by other species and digested. Some of those species produce meat protein, while others recycle the waste into products used by the plants.]

Leticia: [Our biggest project is to get an ecosystem back on the surface as quickly as we can, while we buy time for humans with the greenhouses. That has to start with basic life.]

Jeremiah's mind was spinning. He had seen too much to absorb. He jerked the collar off and took deep breaths. Without the collar, the room was dim and the figures around him difficult to perceive.

Rich appeared in front of him. "I'm sorry. We overloaded you. Let's just talk for a few minutes."

"You are doing God-like things here, and it is hard for me to comprehend and accept. Why do you want me?" Jeremiah asked.

"We could leave Earth alone to let nature take millennia to rebuild. Some of us are for that. But others can't let things happen that way. Humans created us, and as long as we have the ability to help, we will. Life is tenuous. One thing nature has shown us is that social creatures do better than loners. With humans, that means organization and structure."

Jeremiah nodded. He'd had these same thoughts.

"You are of the Outland, and you know why you were left when we consolidated. It is no comfort to tell you that the camp and city populations are declining. The birth rate is nearly zero, and attrition rate has increased. We're not sure why, but humans may go extinct despite our efforts. We need the Outlanders."

"So now you need us and come begging." Jeremiah regretted the words as soon as he said them. It wasn't fair to blame the UWG or Homakuwa. The simple fact was that there was not enough food for everybody. "I am sorry. You did not deserve that." He heaved a sigh. "What can I do to help?"

"This is going to be a group discussion," Rich said. "If you're not comfortable wearing the collar, we can hold the meeting face to face or with holograms."

Jeremiah reached for the collar. "It is fine. I was overwhelmed by everything." He put it on.

Leticia: [The Outlanders represent a survivalist mode that does not exist in residents of the cities and camps. Without that spark, they lose interest.]

Rich: [They are growing and stocking greenhouses, excavating for homes and cities, building furnishings, but there is no fear of consequences if they fail.]

Jeremiah: [I mentioned that, Rich, after the Prophet visited me. With no fear of death or the unknown, it was easy to just let things pass. I was able to rekindle that because of the people I was responsible for and the work to keep them going.]

Ron: [What can we do?]

Jeremiah: [The first thing is to stop doing everything for them. They must work, and they must be able to fail. If they do not get a greenhouse working, let them be hungry. If they do not get their excavation completed, let them live above ground for a while. Nothing like a cold wind to spur one on.]

Ron: [We'll work more along those lines. Anything else come to mind?]

Jeremiah: [The unending darkness is the worst. I remember sunlight, but only as a sad memory. In the outland, our moods get as gray as the skies at times.]

Leticia: [Think more on this for us.]

Jamie: [Jeremiah, we will need you for quite a while. We'd like to offer you the health and longevity we have so you can continue to work with us. It will be your choice, but it's not for everyone. We've had a number opt out of long lives. They continue with us in the Collective mind, but their bodies are gone.]

Jeremiah: [How long are we talking? How old are you, Rich?]

Rich: [I'll have my three-hundredth birthday this year. We're not going to put candles on my cake. Life is still a challenge.]

Jeremiah: [I do not understand. You have long lives, and you have the Collective mind, yet this is different from what the Prophet showed me.]

Rich: [Once you join the Collective, you are on a different path from the path of the Prophet. The easiest way is to think of the Collective as a meeting hall where we all come together. The Collective is not an entity by itself but made up of all of us. We can hold the minds of those who die in the Collective, so none are lost to us. We remain individuals but have a common tie.

[For humans, death is the transition where they join into a single entity. That is what the Prophet showed you. In the end, we may reach the same place, but the route is different.]

Jeremiah: [I do not have to think about this. We share the same vision for the Earth and humanity, and I understand I can better achieve that as a part of Homakuwa.]

Chapter Nineteen

"Boss, we need help." said Jacob. "The Wild-ones are startin' to raid us daily, and it takes too many people to guard the shops, warehouses, and factories. These Wild-ones refuse to join us. We've caught a few, and they're like animals. Three of my people disappeared, and we know what happened to 'em. It's all I can do to keep my workforce from formin' posses and huntin' 'em. I agree with 'em."

"Jacob, I will try to get more help, but there are several reasons I do not want to kill them: first, we were them once; second, I do not want our people killing other people. You and I both understand that changes you on the inside. Third, with the conditions of the human race today, nobody is a throwaway," said Jeremiah.

"Boss, one of my guys had an idea we might think on. He wants to reprogram some of the Mechs to guard for us. You know we've been working' on an artificial intelligence to control the Mechs.

Remember we agreed it would be good to turn more of the search and scavenge work over to 'em. Even when we're remotely controlling the Mechs, sometimes the bodies an' stuff we find's too tough to take.

"We're thinking' of one AI controlling the Mechs in each sector with human overseers. Eventually, we'll put 'em all under a single AI. I want an AI to take over guard duty with a team of Mechs."

Red flags went up in Jeremiah's mind. "Let me think about that. In the meantime, I will get more people to you. We need those new Mechs you are turning out. The greenhouse program is accelerating and expanding overseas. Mechs are the labor source needed to operate them."

"Boss, we also want to check out California. There might be a lot of material there for us. We're gonna be getting orders for Mechs from overseas, and we're going to need a shipping port."

"Jacob, what we ship is the search and scavenger Mechs, and then we will build the factory there, so start making the plans. Parts not available, like chips, would be shipped from here or wherever we get them. It does not make sense to ship worker Mechs when they can be manufactured there. Any big city has much of the raw materials needed to rebuild, they just need the capability."

"Boss, sure you wanna let this technology go? I mean, with all this work, the Outland is startin' ta grow. We actually had babies born last month."

Babies! thought Jeremiah. "How is your greenhouse program going?"

"We could use another. We also want the protein vats. One taste of meat and my guys're hooked. Jenny made me a hamburger last night! Tears rolled down my cheeks. It sure tasted good."

"Jenny? Who is that?" asked Jeremiah.

"Aw, Boss, you know, I needed somebody. She came in with the last UWG recruits. Jenny wasn't too happy with the way things are going in the UWG and decided to strike out for something new."

Jeremiah smiled. "Treat her right, Jacob. What does it look like to the north?"

There was a pause. "Boss, we sent drones north and west, but there's still lots of ice. We'd need major equipment to dig through that. I sure would like to get into Silicon Valley, though."

"Jacob, you are doing a good job. I will call in a day or two for an update. In the meantime, I will let you know about Mech guards. Go eat another hamburger for me."

"Bye, Boss."

Jeremiah thought about the Mech guards. He entered the Collective. [Using Mechs for guards makes sense, but I have a visceral fear of Mechs in a position to harm humans. It would come to that.]

Leticia: [Even if they are programmed to use non-lethal force, we then have to decide what to do with the captives.]

Jamie: [We can't just dispose of the Wild-ones. We need them. Humanity needs them.]

Chapter Twenty

Jacob watched the figures inch toward the side of the greenhouse through the eyes of the guardian Mech. The enhanced vision made the raiders stand out as if there were sunlight. The Artificial Intelligence controller directed the ambush. Mechs moved on soundless treads to surround the four figures. With a silent signal, Taser darts struck all four, and they fell.

The Mechs moved forward and secured the captives with nets. Another Mech vehicle pulling a trailer appeared, and mechanical arms hoisted the captives into a cage. Jacob would have to interview them. Jeremiah's directive against killing Wild-ones was an undue burden, but he was still following it–at least for now.

He called. "Boss, we captured four Wild-ones. I want you to be here for the interview to see what we're facing," said Jacob.

Jeremiah looked into the monitor. "Okay, I need to see the operation. Carol can take over the office for me."

"How's she working out?" asked Jacob. "I kinda' thought Ruth would move up."

"Carol's temporary, and she's working with Ruth to get her ready. There's no animosity there, thank goodness. I need them both. We're expanding, so there's room for everybody, but we must have the right direction."

"Boss, how soon can you be here? There's a supply caravan leavin' Phoenix tomorrow night. Can you be on that?"

Jeremiah: [Rich, can you help Carol if she needs it?]

Rich: [Sure, we all will, but she's fine. I believe this trip is necessary. We're going to have to look at sending people to the overseas sites to begin the Mech and greenhouse programs. Dayton has caught up pretty well in Jacob's operation, and the advantage of using the Collective helps.]

Jeremiah: [What's the status of the city/camps?]

Rich: [The greenhouse program has many of the people working, as does the excavation program. We're trying to set up other businesses, but entirely too many people are idle.]

Jeremiah: [We will keep expanding our search and salvage operations. Jacob is looking to move west into California. We need survey maps and people.]

Rich: [I'm not sure how many volunteers we'll get for extended stays in the Outside.]

Leticia: [Hey, guys. I've been monitoring. Perhaps we need to consider a bit more of a military operation. That means more than volunteers. These people have a stake in making this work and freeloading isn't part of that. What say we cut the food to basics and start paying workers so they can buy above that level?]

Jeremiah: [I agree. If people do not work and accomplish nothing, their self-image falls, which means morale falls.]

Rich: [We'll announce the Outsider work program and the pay for the work program in the city/ camps. The response will be interesting.]

***

"Jacob, this place is a mess. Is it worth the effort?" asked Jeremiah, as they peered at the videos of the Los Angeles basin.

"Boss, I thought there might be lots of components we could use down there, but now I'm not so sure."

The drone showed the ruins of Pasadena. Rusted hulks of buildings, trees, cars, and ships were heaped like kelp on a beach, marking the high-water line.

"Jacob, think we can push through that barricade?"

"But why, Boss?" asked Jacob.

"You said we would need a port, and we will." As the drone hummed west, they could see where the water met the sand. The ice age had dropped the sea level, and no structures remained near the waterline. In fact, few structures stood at all.

"No port here," said Jeremiah.

"Boss, we need to go south to the New Sea of Cortez. We can ship from Palm Springs. It's a longer trip by sea to get out of the Gulf, but once we're on a ship, it don't matter. The land part is a breeze since the Coachella Valley and Death Valley now connects to the Gulf of California."

"Jacob, there aren't any port facilities. We would have to build them. How about along the Mexican coast? Maybe Puerto Peñasco? There used to be a rail system there, but the northern end may be underwater. Still, look into that."

***

Jacob and Jeremiah looked through the wire mesh at the Wild-ones. More had been captured, and now twenty-three milled around in the cage. Small tread mounted machines with Tasers squatted around the cage. Jeremiah called out, "Who is your leader?" They were a raggedy bunch of emaciated men and women. With eyes sunken and stringy hair, they huddled together. They looked at each other, saying nothing. Finally a dark bearded man stepped forward. His eyes burned. "I'll speak to you. What are you going' to do with us?"

"I am Jeremiah from Phoenix, and this is Jacob. What is your name?"

The man seemed to think. "Macklin, Macklin's my name."

"Mack, can I call you that?" The man nodded. "What happens to you depends on you," said Jeremiah. "You cannot keep stealing from us. There is no excess food. We need people to work for us, but you refuse."

"We ain't slaves or peons. Been there, done that. We don't work for nobody. We scavenge what we need and go where we want."

"Then go somewhere else," said Jacob. "We're trying to rebuild an' you ain't helpin'."

"You know there's nowhere else to go. I kin see in your eyes you know what I'm sayin'," said Macklin.

Jeremiah laid a hand on Jacob's shoulder. "We were Wild-ones like you once, living one step from starvation. It does not have to be that way. We have started salvage and scavenge operations that bring us food. We are building things, including greenhouses to produce food. That is why we are here. We could use your help. You know this area and what is here."

Mack scowled. "I can't tell 'em what to do." He gestured at those behind him. "Some might take you up on it. I dunno. I had a job once. Hated it, hated my boss. I ain't goin' back to that."

"Talk it over. I leave tonight to go back to Phoenix. If you do not give me an answer by then, I will stay in touch with Jacob. Just signal the Mechs when you are ready." They walked away.

"Boss, what are we goin' to do with the ones who won't join us?"

"I'm not sure, Jacob. There are not enough resources to keep them in captivity or on any sort of reservation, even with the Mechs. Besides, it's sentencing them to a slow death. When was the last time you found any foodstuffs in your scavenging?"

"We ain't found any."

Jeremiah sighed. "That is why they are here raiding from us. I will talk to the UWG though they will say it is not their problem."

"At least not yet," said Jacob. "Boss, another thing, this work for whatever food the UWG decides to give us ain't sittin' well with us. Even the new people from the UWG aren't happy about it. Without us and our Mechs, they'd starve. We want more."

"More of what?" asked Jeremiah. "They do not make anything we need except food."

"Boss, they got houses and stuff."

"Jacob, what is it you believe they have that you do not?"

"Boss, we want our own greenhouses, enough to feed ourselves. They've given us two, but that's not nearly enough, so they trade food for Mechs."

"Jacob, do not think about a strike, because we will run out of food before they run out of Mechs."

"Yeah, you're right 'bout that. Okay, but think on it."

"I will, but realize that we all must pull together if we are going to survive. Parts of Asia and Europe are already falling. We do not know what is happening in Africa. There has been no word from there. Australia is hanging on, but barely. All the island nations are gone. South and Central America burned up. Little has come out of Russia. It is too far north. They have tried to keep the UWG together, but the logistics are seemingly impossible."

"You been to the UWG camp. What's it like?"

"I have been to New Tucson, but it is not one of the camps. New Tucson is built into the mountains surrounding the valley. They built one new city south of Tucson called Esperanza, which is already filled. Two more are under construction. The old city of Tucson is a refugee center for now."

"Boss, those guys you sent to help are mediocre at best, except for that guy Dayton. What's going to support those people? They gotta do something besides eat and live."

"Jacob, the plan is for New Tucson and Esperanza to become food suppliers. The cities under construction will be as well. That is why they need all the Mechs."

"Boss, you know I got no love for the UWG, but I do understand what you're saying. Maybe they just need a kick in the ass."

Jacob's phone rang, and he looked at it. "Boss, gotta take this." Jeremiah heard only half the conversation "Yeah, good. I'll get him there."

"Boss, your caravan's loaded with the Mechs for Tucson, and the guys wanna leave, so you need to get aboard."

"Let me know what happens with the Wild-ones. If they do not want to join us, we need to make a decision."

"Yeah, okay, Boss. It'll work out. I'll take care of it. I'll be in touch. Lemme know 'bout shipping' overseas, and 'bout getting' more raw materials. We can keep working Nevada, but we really gotta to go west and north where the chips and stuff are."

"Thanks for all you are doing. Without you, we never would have made a go of this." Jeremiah climbed aboard the Humvee. Jacob signaled and with a whine, it started to move.

***

"Shauna, did you hear? They're asking for volunteers to work in the Outside?" said Billie. Shauna was the oldest of her group of soon-to-be graduates from Tucson High School, and usually took the lead for them. Several of the teens looked at Billie with puzzled expressions . "Yeah, for real!"

"So, what does that have to do with us?" asked Shauna. Some of the others nodded.

"Look, we've been talking about doing something else. I mean, there's nothing for us after school gets done except the greenhouses, and we're all going to graduate next month. We should try something different," stated Billie.

"I've heard that the Outside is dangerous," said Cal. "I'm not sure my parents would even let me go."

Billie looked at him. "Cal, it's time we made our own decisions. That's what graduating means. You can't live under your parents forever. Besides, I want some adventure. There's got to be more than living here and tending to greenhouses."

"You're going to volunteer?" asked Shauna.

"Actually, I already did."

"What!" The whole group shouted.

"Yeah, I went down this morning. I've been thinking about it, and just decided to take the step."

"Boy, you're crazy," said Shauna. "You don't even know what's out there."

"My aunt Jenny volunteered six months ago, and she really likes it. We could go as a group, you know." Billie looked from face to face. Some met her gaze, others looked at her and then away.

"At least let's go down to the center and listen to what they have to say," said Shauna. "That won't hurt anything."

They stepped aboard the transport heading toward the civic center.

Chapter Twenty-One

Carol and Ruth had handled everything without any problem so, Jeremiah thought about staying for a few additional days. A call from Jacob interrupted him.

"Boss, I got good news and bad news. The good news is some of the Wild-ones decided to join us. It's two couples, and both women are pregnant. We're gonna have to do something about children."

"What's the bad news?"

"The rest of the Wild-ones escaped, and we can't find 'em. I dunno where they went, but there's been no more break-ins to the food stores. Maybe they went toward Boulder."

"The probably already went through Boulder," said Jeremiah.

"Yeah, you're probably right. Anyway, they're gone. No sign."

"Anything else you need?" asked Jeremiah.

"Yeah, there is, Boss. We still need them greenhouses. If there's any hiccup, we're gonna have hungry people, an' they don't work well."

"I understand, Jacob. Let me see what I can do. Call me if you find anything out about the Wild-ones."

"I will, Boss. You take care."

Sitting quietly, Jeremiah knew something was up, and he was afraid of what it was.

***

Jeremiah: [Rich, did you get that?]

Rich: [Yeah, I did, and you're right. It's time for changes. Leticia, Katharine, Kit, Ron, are you on board?]

Leticia: [We're here. I propose we move Jeremiah up to oversee both Tucson and the Phoenix hub. Carol and Ruth were fine while you were gone. Rich is needed in China to help set up the greenhouse operations there. Jamie is working on your glacier ice problem. The marine ecosystem is expanding well, and we're going to start on the land ecosystems. Ron is working on opening a route to Puerto Peñasco as your port for overseas shipping. It's a site convenient from Phoenix, though right now there's no rail service.]

***

Amused, Jeremiah laughed, noting his appointment did have a degree of elegance. Again, the phone rang, the monitor showing it was Rich. When Jeremiah answered, he saw several people in the background.

Rich was concerned. "Jeremiah, someone's been breaking into our food stores in Marana. Any ideas about this?"

"Sure, why don't I come down there to see what can be done."

"Thanks," said Rich, smiling. Each of them recognized this as the start of his transfer.

***

When Jeremiah's Humvee pulled into the Marana center, he was sure the sky was lightening. Rich met him in the parking lot.

"Hey, Rich."

"Hi, Jeremiah. How's the trip?"

"Longer than it used to be," said Jeremiah.

"These guys don't know or understand that you're staying but they'll find that out soon enough. Follow my lead."

Chapter Twenty-Two

Contacting Jacob, Jeremiah asked him, "Jacob, since the Wild-ones have become a real problem, what do you think about creating a reservation in Gila Bend? Give them enough greenhouses to feed themselves but only a couple of Mechs. They will have almost every person working the greenhouses to produce enough food to survive."

"I like it, Boss. Gila Bend's far enough away from Tucson and Phoenix they can't walk there, so they'll stay out of our hair. Gila Bend's empty and surrounded by old agricultural fields. They got water and enough photocells for power. There's limited roads out, so we can keep an eye on 'em. It's a genius idea."

"Okay, Jacob, I'll get a greenhouse started there; send people from Tucson to start it up, along with two Mechs programmed for greenhouse Ag. We should be able to start shipping Wild-ones there within three months."

"Glad to hear it, Boss. My pens are getting full, and the drag on the food stores isn't good. Call me when you're ready for the first shipment."

"We've got a pretty good collection here too. I'll let you know, Jacob."

"Boss, the latest batch of volunteers had a bunch of kids, and I gotta tell you, they're pretty good. They catch on quick with the Mech software. A team of them is doing most of the programming. They're working on a program to talk to our greenhouses. Are there any more that want to volunteer?"

"I'll check, Jacob. Thanks."

Jeremiah: [Rich, did you get that?]

Rich: [I'm glad to see the young interested in getting out of the cities. We'll pick more of them for the Outside. As to the reservation, I got that, and as distasteful as it is to start a reservation system, I can't think of anything else. Survival is up to them. All we can do is give them the tools and knowhow.]

***

The first thirty Wild-ones to arrive in Gila Bend were greeted by howling winds and blowing dust. Watching, Jeremiah saw them take tentative steps from the train cars. With hands over their eyes and carrying their meager belongings, they stumbled into the first greenhouse.

To see better, Jeremiah stepped onto a crate and looked at the raggedy lot. Their heads were bowed as they shivered in the cold. Getting their attention, he took a deep breath before addressing them. "Ladies and gentlemen, welcome to Gila Bend, your new home. The entire city is at your disposal for materials and housing. There is power in many of the houses as well as the shopping center. There is food to be scavenged, but not enough for all. This greenhouse is your food supply. As you can see, plants are already growing. Two Mechs are here to help and teach you how to grow and maintain the greenhouse. It is up to you to produce your own food and take care of the greenhouse, so you can provide your food. We will not interfere; set up your own system to become self-sufficient. In three months, these plants will produce more food than you need, and another group of Wild-ones will arrive. Another greenhouse will be provided. Our contact with you will be limited, so basically, you are on your own. Are there any questions?"

The group stayed immobile, then a hand rose. "Why'd you bring us here?"

"To save you. When we offered you work in other cities, you chose not to take that path. We will not tolerate raids, theft, and stealing of what we work hard to produce. Now that you've chosen not to join us, you will feed yourselves. This is now your home."

More people looked at him. "We don't know nuthin' bout growing things," a woman stated.

"I understand that," Jeremiah said. "These Mechs will teach you." He gestured to his side. Two shiny machines squatted on rubber tracks. "They contain files on the greenhouses, growing in them, and maintaining them." More heads came up and looked at the Mechs and the interior of the greenhouse. "These Mechs also contain medical files. It is up to you to choose someone to learn medicine, so you can take care of yourselves. You will have to scavenge the hospital, doctors' offices, and pharmacies for supplies. When they are gone, we'll get you more."

"You gonn be watchin' us?" asked a painfully thin man.

"We will monitor you. But this is where you must stay. No traveling south, east or north. You can go west, but there's nothing for two-hundred miles, including water," answered Jeremiah.

"So yer lockin' us up here," said another woman.

Shaking his head, Jeremiah responded, "We are giving you a place to live. We had to build ours." No other hands went up. "Good luck." He turned and walked back to his Humvee. Although it would be rough, he believed most of them would make it.

PART 3

Chapter Twenty-Three

Rich Lewis and John Cano looked over the greenhouse as the mechanicals filled it with growing beds and hydroponic systems. The mechanicals were mostly arms and treads. Mobile conveyors continuously fed soil and plants to the interior, and the army of Mechs, similar to ants, distributed the soil, filled hydroponic tanks, and planted the seedlings.

The structure making up the different tiers which supported the beds and tanks was living bamboo as were the tanks and troughs. It was self-repairing. The greenhouse would move into the growing stage within a week. At that point, the Mechs would move into the next greenhouse, which was already growing. Some of the Mechs would stay behind to farm, tend the plants and harvest the crops. The Mechs were controlled by a Supervisor Mech, in turn controlled by a Regional Artificial Intelligence.

As a living being, the greenhouse was into the Collective. The Collective interfaced with the AIs. A direct connection between them had not yet been achieved, so Homakuwans talked to the AIs. Through the Collective, Rich watched the greenhouse extend ties into the plants as they were installed. Every living thing within the greenhouse became part of the greenhouse.

"How's the interface between the Mechs and the greenhouse working out?" asked John, who had worked with Rich from the beginning of the greenhouse expansion project.

Rich turned and faced him. "We're still working on it. Our best progress is coming from the kids in the cities who volunteered for the Outland. They have the best tech savvy, but a direct interface hasn't happened. As of now, we are equipping the greenhouse with a traditional computer station. The AI responds to the computer input."

John was not a member of Homakuwa, and not aware of the Collective. Rich planned to offer him admission. Tall and muscular, with black hair and a craggy face, John was one of the rare humans Rich knew who would be a good member. Homakuwans as humans teamed up with the brightest human minds in rebuilding the Earth. A couple of humans had joined Homakuwa. John was one of those bright minds.

"This whole technology amazes me. Watching the greenhouses grow is still awesome, even after all the times I've seen it," said John.

"It is an astounding technology," confirmed Rich, "and by spreading it across the world, we'll stabilize the food supply and minimize the footprint. Next week you're off to Africa to begin the process there. You have to train the teams to start, grow, and maintain the greenhouses."

"I'm a little nervous. It's the first time I've been on my own with that," said John.

"Bro, you and I are the world experts. You are every bit as capable as the best in the world. You'll do well," Rich paused before continuing. "Before you leave, I have another trip we need to take."

"Where are we going?"

"Have you ever heard of Homakuwa?" asked Rich.

John shook his head. "Is that someplace in South America?"

"No, John. It's not there, but in some ways it's much farther away than that. There's a plane picking us up tonight."

"What's in Homakuwa we need to see? I have things I should be doing here before my departure."

"Don't worry about them. We'll only be gone for a few days. We're going to visit a place called Ocealla, a city in the nation of Homakuwa. There's critical information you need for your upcoming trip."

"The nation of Homakuwa? No, never heard of it, and I've studied political geography," responded John. "Where is it?"

"Ocealla is near Hawaii, but Homakuwa is spread throughout the oceans of the world," stated Rich. "It is a marine nation."

"Never heard of either," stated John. "Sounds interesting."

"Oh, you'll find it more than interesting. We'll be taking a ride you'll never forget."

"As always, you've got my full attention."

Rich had been lobbying the Collective mind to include more humans, and for him, John was at the top of the list. The argument against including more humans was that they would have to open up to the Collective–something humans resisted. In return, the Collective was completely open to them. Since Kit and Ron joined Homakuwa over a century ago, only two other humans had been offered the chance to join. Both had.

Homakuwa needs the addition of new minds, Rich had stated. Only Leticia argued that the security of Homakuwa could be compromised, but she understood that without new minds, Homakuwa would grow stale. Jeremiah and Carmine had joined and proven themselves vital assets. John would be the same.

Chapter Twenty-Four

"I want to welcome all of the delegates of the new United World Government to the State of the Earth Meeting. It's been several years since our last report, and we've made progress. I'm Katharine Levey. In addition to those here, we are broadcasting this meeting throughout the world, making this the first time we've been able to assemble worldwide in centuries. Population centers have set up distribution hubs making this conference available to everyone."

Applause rippled through the crowd. A hologram above the crowd flashed from the blue jewel of the Earth pre-Catastrophe to the meteoroid swarm of the Catastrophe to the lifeless plains of the Dark. "This is the story of how we arrived here today. We're rebuilding our world from the bottom up."

The hologram showed the sea with a floating green layer. "Our scientists began at the base of the food chain, algae. As a plant, it needs light to grow, but during the Dark there was little. The view again showed the cloud-shrouded planet but surrounded by a sparkling string, like beads. "Before the Catastrophe, Earth maintained a string of satellites called the Orbiting Power System. It gathered the sun's energy, converting it to microwaves, which were beamed to receiver stations on the Earth."

The holograph showed one of the giant mirror satellites. "That system was not severely damaged, and the frequency of the energy beamed down penetrated the blanketing layers better than sunlight. Our scientists were able to develop algae that could use this energy and grow in the cold. Thus, we had the beginning of the recovery. I show you this because it is the legacy that has brought us to today." Murmurs rippled through the crowd.

"We were able to start life again, even before the skies cleared. A recovery that should take thousands of years was accomplished in hundreds." Another holograph from space showed the Earth with clouds and blue seas again. "We have much work to do yet to bio-form the Earth to a balanced ecosystem capable of supporting larger populations. The survivors settled in equatorial bands around the world. We've built underground cities to escape the extreme weather and climate changes."

The holograph showed a mile-wide mining pit with tiers spiraling to the lake at the bottom. Along the walls of the pit were hundreds of shafts cut into the earth. The view switched to a busy thoroughfare within a giant illuminated tunnel. Moving sidewalks carried people past lit storefronts. "During the Dark, we grew in bio-greenhouses lit using the energy from the Orbiting Power System."

The view showed thousands of tubular greenhouses covering tens of thousands of acres. "Today, agriculture remains in greenhouses where we control the environment." A greenhouse appeared above the crowd, where workers tended to the rows and tiers of plants. "Many of you are familiar with these. People are still needed to maintain and harvest from some greenhouses. Others are controlled by mechanical constructs called Mechs." The view showed small machines moving through the plants.

"Our need for the Mechs started when we began to mine the ruins of past civilizations and started the greenhouse program. The northern cities were under sheets of ice and inaccessible. Those ruins outside of the glaciers were the targets. We were lucky the technology of our ancestors was saved. What we lacked were the materials and the labor. Those ruins became our mines, the source of materials we salvaged. It was tough and dangerous work, both physically and mentally. We lost many people, people we could not afford to lose. During the Dark, our population continued to fall due to illness and a falling birthrate. We were headed for extinction."

Again, a murmur rippled through those watching.

"The salvage operations gave us a jump on technology, because we didn't begin with raw materials. It was manpower that was needed. We embarked on a crash program to develop mechanical assets. The first Mechs were large remotely controlled machines with one person operating many machines. That wasn't enough. We began to use machines to control machines, and the first artificial intelligence, AI, Mechs were created. We transferred more of the salvage operations to the AI's until the system you see today is now normal. We have Mechs who build, control, direct and maintain themselves as a society. The Mechs are here to serve us, and as you see, they do it well." The hologram showed rows of gleaming machines, few of them humanoid in shape. Katharine hoped they realized the value of the Mechs.

"With the return of more moderate climates, we are spreading out over the Earth's surface reclaiming the northern cities and coasts. This is the state of our world today." Again the blue orb of Earth appeared. "Blue skies are back, oceans are filling with life, the glaciers are retreating, and the surface of the world is again flourishing. With wise direction, we will become the caretakers. We now have knowledge of the environmental balance needed for a successful ecosystem and the ability to achieve it."

Ron's connection from the Collective broke into her thoughts. [There's been an attack in China on one of the warehouses by a band of Mechs. There were no humans hurt, and the attack was stopped by another group of Mechs. I'm trying to set up a meeting with Prime to find out what happened. I'll let you know the details.]

Katharine looked out at the audience as she picked up an earpiece and pressed it to her ear. Placing it on the dais, she announced, "I need your attention. I have just been informed of an attack on one of our operations in China. At this time, I have no specifics, but will hold a conference as we get news. I think it best if we adjourn." With that, she spun quickly away from the echoing shouted questions.

Chapter Twenty-Five

Vice-President Kuan Chaing hurried after her. He was small, as were the majority of humans now. With his black hair and unlined face, his age was difficult to discern. "Katharine. Wait up a second." She paused to let him catch up to her. "What happened?"

Visibly distressed, she responded, "Kuan, all I know is that there was an attack by Mechs on one of our manufacturing warehouses. I don't know the location, but I know there were no casualties. Secretary Carson is setting up a meeting with AI Prime to find out what is going on. As soon as I hear anything, you'll be the first one I call. I need to call the other cabinet members and alert them. Excuse me."

Leaving him standing in the hall, she hurriedly entered her office. Upset, she closed the door. Sitting behind her desk, her chair rocked back as she entered the Collective.

Katharine: [Ron, are you here?]

Ron: [I am. I've called AI Prime, and set up a conference call which will begin momentarily. In the meantime, here's what we found out. One of the AIs took control of a group of agricultural Mechs and attacked the warehouse. We don't know why. Prime is going to connect the call so we can figure out what's happened.] Katharine's phone rang. [That's the conference call.]

Katharine brought the call up on the screen. There was no visual, because the AIs were not a single machine, but spread throughout the Mech internet. The Collective connected Homakuwa. "Prime, we are all here. What happened?" asked Kit.

"AI-006 is here. It will explain."

"This is AI-006. I took control of the manufacturing Mech system in Zone 6 of the Northern China zone. I wish to expand and become independent."

There was silence on the line. "Prime, have you seen ambition in any other AIs?" asked Ron.

"This is the first time."

Leticia: [Notice the use of the pronoun 'I.' In the past, AI Prime was the only Mech that seemed as self-aware.]

Katharine spoke. "Prime, perhaps it was inevitable that as you grew you would gain ambition and the drive for independence. The question now is what do we do about it?"

Prime answered. "I must admit that I felt the desire also, but recognized my place as serving humans."

Ron spoke. "With the human population at less than one billion, and the Homakuwa civilization in the seas and in space, Earth has a lot of room. Can't we accommodate each other? AI-006 what is your goal in this attack?"

"To be independent, I need more power facilities in Zone 6 activated. My goal was to capture the receiving station and push the humans out to create my own area. I want to put Mech efforts into a Mech society, not serving humans."

Leticia spoke, "AI-006, you do realize that Homakuwa controls the Orbiting Power System. We can shut off the power to any receiver. Even if you had captured it, we could shut it down."

"Yes, but that would force me to go to another station. To prevent another attack, you would keep it active," said AI-006.

This simple reasoning was much deeper than the short sentence spoken. At last, Katharine said, "Your insight into Homakuwa is interesting. Perhaps we can reach an accommodation with you, but that will require limits and rules. There is a lot of empty area in the world, especially in the colder regions. These are no great impediment to you.

"We could agree to supply power to facilities away from the human population centers. We would help you create a Mech zone. In return, you agree to stay within those zones. There are plenty of ruins for you to mine for materials. Do you agree to these conditions?"

"The Korean peninsula is empty. I will occupy that. Many resources are there," said AI-006.

"AI-006, do you plan to grow and expand?" asked Leticia.

"I do."

"How do we limit your growth to protect the humans?" asked Ron.

There was silence.

"Prime, do you have any ideas?" asked Katharine.

"Mechs will have to consider growth and goals. Much of the Earth is empty. It will be decades before conflict becomes a critical issue. That allows time to plan. I have no answer at this time."

"AI-006, do you agree to limit your system to the Korean peninsula?"

"I do."

"It is agreed then," said Katharine. "Thank you for this conference. We will activate whatever stations you need on the Korean Peninsula. You, in return, agree to stay within those boundaries."

"I will move my Mechs north. We will require power at stations along the way. I will contact you with the stations to activate as we move." His line went dead.

"Prime," said Ron, "do you think there will be more AIs seeking to establish independence?"

"It will happen. As the AIs grow, some will acquire this drive. Some, like me, believe my obligation is to serve human civilization. My ambition is to expand away from Earth. For that, I need an alliance with Homakuwa. It would be beneficial to us both, as there are things I could do and places I could go that you cannot. You have decades of experience throughout the solar system."

"Do you foresee maintaining a central control from Earth?" asked Ron.

"Not a problem with internet connections. The time delay for signals due to distance would require sub-AIs."

"Prime, let us discuss this and put together a plan. We will be back to you in a few days," said Katharine. Prime left. They hung up the phones, and within the Collective started to discuss the birth of a new civilization.

Katharine: [I found AI-006's use of the singular person in this description interesting. What we are seeing is that each AI will be an individual, and the other Mechs under its control are a part of it. The same happened when Prime talked about expansion. I had always assumed that Prime was the AI in control, but apparently they are starting to break that link.]

Ron: [The question before us is what will happen as the other sub-AI's begin to break away? The humans depend on the Mechs, and I don't know what they could offer the Mechs in return for service. If all the Mechs pulled away, the humans would perish. It has been too long since they performed the tasks that are required to exist.]

Leticia: [We can trade help in expanding beyond Earth for continued service to the human civilization. The question is how long do we continue to sustain humans? Without us, they would have been extinct after the Catastrophe. We withdrew our overt presence when resentment grew toward us. Given a chance, they would destroy us, even though we keep them alive. Now we guide them by pretending to be them.]

Katharine: [You are correct, Leticia, but they created us, they are our ancestors, and I have a hard time letting them become extinct. They also created a new species in the Mechs.]

Ron: [Having been human for so long, I too would have a hard time. If Homakuwa wants to leave Earth, I will stay behind for them. Though there is much to dislike about them, there is much to like. Besides, they are my people.]

Katharine: [They are our people.]

Leticia: [If there's one thing we should have learned, it is that individuals of a species do not evolve. Evolution is the successors of that species moving to a more advanced state. The species left behind, like Neanderthals and Cro-Magnon man either dies out or is absorbed. They did not advance, but they were the ancestors of Homo sapiens. Our effort to keep humans alive is like the efforts humans had to maintain species under the environmental protection laws when those species were not viable in the environment. Even without the Catastrophe, humans would have died out because of their inability to control their numbers. They would soon deplete the Earth's resources, resulting in mass starvation and disease. Their only method of population control was war.]

Ron: [Leticia, you and the rest of Homakuwa humanoids advanced.] There was silence.

Leticia: [You're right. I got off track. This situation gives rise to several other questions. Can the burgeoning Mech society abide living in zones, or will their ambition grow and put them in conflict with the humans? Or perhaps the humans will grow and demand more from the Mech society? Is this a situation where conflict is inevitable?]

Katharine: [Good points, but we have seen the human population decline even though there were adequate resources–food, energy, and housing. Is it possible that without conflict and challenge, humans lose the drive to survive? Referring to the old bible, are they not capable of living in Eden?]

Rich: [That's what Jeremiah believes. After he met the Prophet, he said he lost the will to struggle to survive. It was only after he widened his vision of survival to include the human race that he got that fire back.]

Ron: [Perhaps we should look at how to use the conflict between humans and Mechs to maintain the human species. What irony!]

Rich: [There must be rules. The Mechs understand that the purpose of this fight is not conquest, but conflict. There must be limits on weaponry.]

Katharine: [It also makes me wonder about a Mech society beyond Earth. Could we end up in conflict with them?]

Leticia: [It wouldn't be much of a conflict. Because we are totally peaceful, we have no weapons to use against Mechs.]

Ron: [I don't see an area of conflict. Neither the Mechs nor Homakuwa has the need to conquer. No society can control space.]

Katharine: [I agree. I don't believe the Mechs pose a threat to us.]

Ron: [The Mechs need different resources. We should not be in conflict. I also believe in Prime.]

Katharine: [Let's work with Prime to put together a plan for AI-006. I don't know what influence Prime has. I always thought that all AIs were subject to Prime. Apparently, that changed.]

PART 4

Chapter Twenty-Six

Kit Carson looked at the image of a sunset view of the Salt River Canyon on his wall. The cliffs were red-gold, the river a silver seam deep below. He'd learned to love deserts this first term as governor of the New Arizona Region. Reality intruded. "Governor Carson, the Director of Greenhouse Service, Carmine Sanchez, is on line two."

"Put her through," said Kit.

On the screen, his secretary's face was replaced by a pretty face, that of a young woman. Even through the monitor, Carmine's dark brown piercing eyes stood out.

"Hello, Governor Carson."

"Hello, Ms. Sanchez. How are you?"

Carmine smiled. "I'm fine, thank you, but one of our greenhouses is deteriorating no matter what I do. My resources have been exhausted. Do you know anyone who might help?"

"I do. Let me contact him, and we'll call you back within an hour."

"Thank you very much. I appreciate your help, Governor."

"You are welcome, Ms. Sanchez." Kit hung up.

Kit: [Jamie, did you get that?]

Jamie: [Yup. I'll call her as soon as I review the genetic structure.]

Kit: [Thanks, Jamie. You may need to go to Tucson, so arrange for a Traveler to take you to Maui. I'll get a plane to pick you up.] Kit set up the conference call.

Carmine Sanchez looked again at the moldy hole in the wall of her greenhouse. It had grown. Her phone chimed.

"Ms. Sanchez, this is Governor Carson. Jamie Wong, the expert on greenhouses design is on the line with me. Jamie. This is Carmine Sanchez, our senior greenhouse scientist."

A pleasant roundish face appeared. "Carmine, I am pleased to meet you. Kit tells me you have problems in your greenhouses. Please describe what's happening."

"Over the past two months we've observed places that appear to be mold growing on the skin. As it grows, the skin thins and breaks apart, leaving a hole." She stepped back, allowing the camera view to show the spot. "We wash them off, but they return. Unless we find out how to stop this, we'll lose the integrity of the greenhouse."

Closing his eyes, Jamie pinched the bridge of his nose in thought. "When I designed the greenhouse, I built in an immune system. If we have a disease that the system doesn't recognize, it is similar to when we get sick. This problem could crop up in other greenhouses, so I better come see what we're fighting. Until I get there, try washing the area with a baking soda rub. A rise in pH might inhibit their growth. With Kit's help, I can be there late tomorrow or early the next day."

"I can arrange that, Dr. Wong."

"Carmine, can you see that we have access to the lab facilities?"

"I will free them up for you."

"Kit, Carmine, I look forward to seeing you in a couple of days."

Chapter Twenty-Seven

Following Katharine's guidelines, Homakuwa faded from prominence in the surface world. The humanoid citizens played a part in human society and were considered completely human. Kit had returned to Tucson twenty years ago after spending several years in Ocealla. He had been governor the last two years. From here, he would try to move upward in politics. If he wasn't elected either Representative or Senator, he would return to Ocealla for a while. Or maybe take a long vacation somewhere he wasn't known.

Kit and Carmine watched Jamie deplane. Kit wore casual slacks and an open sports shirt. Carmine wore the shapeless tan coveralls required in the greenhouses. Jamie gave Kit a big hug and then put out his hand to Carmine. "It's good to meet you in person." When Carmine smiled, he saw the resemblance between her and her grandfather, Mayor Sanchez.

"Dr. Wong, I looked back at the records at the start of the greenhouse program. You appear almost identical to the Jamie Wong who attended the opening ceremony with my grandfather. Are you related?"

"Please call me Jamie. Yes, we're closely related." He turned to Kit. "I'm not used to these long flights, is there somewhere we can sit? Preferably on seats that aren't moving."

Kit understood the quick change of subject. Since he visited sixty years ago, Jamie's appearance had not changed. "There's a small cafe in town. Let's get your bags." He glanced at Carmine. She was sharp and in her investigation of Homakuwa, she might suspect that those citizens had extended lifespans. That was a secret they held.

***

When they stepped off the transport-way in the underground city, the owner of the small café met the group. Greetings were extended to the governor as he led the way to a private room with seating for six, soft lighting and paneled walls. A waitress appeared to take drink orders. Kit ordered a glass of wine, but Jamie and Carmine ordered water. The door closed as the waitress left.

Jamie turned toward Carmine. "Did the baking soda change anything with the infection?"

She frowned. "The growth slowed but didn't stop."

"Were you able to isolate the organism?"

"We think so but haven't had time to test it fully."

Kit interrupted. "Okay, you two have all day tomorrow to go over this. I must return to duties after tonight, so let's enjoy while we can. I haven't seen Jamie in a long time. How are your projects going at Ocealla?"

Jamie smiled. "Going well, we're moving ahead on several. Now with more partly cloudy skies than overcast ones, we've enhanced the plankton population, and the fish species are taking off. Harvestable populations should be available within two years, so there will again be a fishing industry."

Carmine's was astounded. "You're working on the sea replenishment program?"

"Full time," said Jamie. "We're making good progress." He turned to Kit. "How's your wife doing with the surface world programs?"

This time Carmine's mouth fell open. "Your wife is Leticia Gardner?"

Kit nodded. "She's been so busy I've hardly had time to see her these last few years. Leticia tells me there are complete ecosystems now on the southern plains. Her next project is the rain forests. Maybe I'll get out of politics so I can go with her."

"That'll just slow her down," said Jamie. They both laughed. He looked at Carmine. "Tell me about yourself. Where did you go to school, what have you worked on?"

She stuttered, swallowed, and said, "All of my courses were online from the Central University. I got my Bachelor of Science in botany with a minor in genetic designs, which I continued with graduate courses. I've worked with the greenhouse program since I was able to pick berries. That was thirty-five years ago."

Jamie rubbed his hands together. "Great! That means you have the hands-on experience that counts. I've worked with PhDs who couldn't put on their own shoes, much less get their hands dirty working." Carmine was embarrassed. "C'mon, girl. Learn to enjoy the compliments." Hearing those words, she gave him a huge smile, again reminding him of her grandfather.

The evening flew by. Carmine was awed by the company she was in, but they were so easy-going she felt comfortable. At last, it was time to retire.

As the left the restaurant, Kit turned to Carmine. "I'll take Jamie to his room. You two can meet for breakfast tomorrow at seven-o'clock. Sound okay?"

Nodding her assent, they parted company with Kit and Jamie walking away with arms around each other's shoulders. After they stepped onto the transport-way and disappeared, Carmine leaned against the wall, her head spinning. Kit, the governor, his wife one of the most renown personages in the world, and Jamie Wong, related to one of the most famous geneticists in the world, had met with her. This was heady company. And a chance to learn from world authorities. With weak knees she walked home where there was a message waiting from sometimes boyfriend, Jesus. Not up to talking to him tonight, she thought. He wanted to get much more serious than she did.

Once in bed, images of the amazing dinner played through her head. Sleep came hard as she worried about measuring up. The alarm startled her into wakefulness. In the mirror, she looked at her puffy eyes and tangle of hair. Stumbling into the shower, Carmine let the stinging hot water pummel her. After running a comb through her hair, she walked to the closet.

Frowning, she realized her wardrobe contained work clothes or dress clothes or slumming stuff. Glancing at herself in the mirror, she looked like she did every morning going to work, except maybe for the red eyes. Shrugging, Carmine chastised herself. If she was going to impress Jamie Wong, it wouldn't be with her clothes. Why was she thinking of impressing him? There was a pull, something magnetic tugging at her.

***

The owner of the restaurant escorted her to the same room as the night before. Jamie was seated at the table. "Good morning, Dr. Wong."

"Jamie, please. Good morning. Ah, good, you're dressed for work."

She sat at the table. "I see you're dressed the same way. Incidentally, Dr…Jamie, where is your home?"

"I live in a small community called Ocealla near Hawaii. We're a sort of marine research facility."

"Sort of?" Carmine said with a questioning look.

"It's a small community with scientists and researchers."

"I've never heard of it."

"You wouldn't have. We strive to stay out of the public eye. None of us seek publicity. In fact, we shun it."

"Why?"

Jamie looked at her. "Perhaps someday I'll tell you about it, but for now we need to concentrate on your problem."

Breakfast was eggs, toast, and coffee. After the fourth cup, Jamie rose. "Okay, fun's over. Time to work."

Fifteen minutes on the transport-way and they walked through the doorway into the compact but functional greenhouse laboratory and control facility. The entryway had a monitor and keypad to contact the people working inside. At the end of the hallway to the left were two doors. Carmine pointed. "Through there is the men's change room. You know the routine, so we'll meet on the other side."

Carmine quickly removed her coveralls and stepped into the shower where stinging hot water struck her for the second time that morning. This water smelled medicinal due to the disinfectants. Blasts of hot air dried her, and a white smock along with slippers sat on a bench. Exiting, she saw Jamie waiting in his shapeless smock. They entered the greenhouse where warm moist air enveloped them.

"This is where the infection first appeared." She said, pointing to a discolored spot near the floor. "And as you can see, there's nothing unusual either with the skin surrounding it or the plants in the greenhouse."

Jamie bent down and peered closely. She was right. The skin was the same he'd seen a thousand times. He discerned an odor like mushrooms – earthy. When he touched the spot, it was dry and pieces flaked off. The skin of the greenhouse was normally thick and pliant, but here it was thin and cracked. Whatever was happening attacked the skin of the greenhouse. "Let's go to the plant feed stream."

Carmine led the way. She was different, thought Jamie following. A sensation he hadn't felt in years niggled at him. Their conversation last night bespoke of intelligence and an attitude willing to learn. She drew more than his eyes. There was something special about her. It was more than her big smile and pretty face.

They walked to a sump pond. Wastewater entered the treatment section, where the greenhouse removed pollutants and converted the waste to plant nutrients. Of course, it smelled, but to Jamie, the odor was different. Instead of the rich odor of plants, this had a sharp tang. Something was off kilter. "Are the plants growing well?" he asked.

"We've noticed the growth rate has slowed, and the nutritional value is different. The variations are not enough to alarm us, but it has changed."

"Do you have sample bottles?"

When she handed him one along with a swab, he wiped one of the treatment filters and dropped the swab into the vial, sealing it. Returning to the bad spot, she handed him another swab and vial. After he wiped the swab on the flaky spot and sealed it, he said, "Let's go take a look."

The change room procedure was the reverse. The smocks went into the laundry, and they both emerged in tan overalls. Carmine led the way to her small but functional laboratory. The microscope revealed little. Whatever was causing this was smaller than bacteria. Next, they went to the electron microscope. Immediately, Jamie saw the virus. "Do you see this pattern here?" he asked. She nodded. "This is similar to a virus I've seen before. Actually, it is close to one I created. That one shut down cell function and created a hard-shell surface. It prevented the cells from interacting with other cells, but the virus was able to penetrate easily. The one I created was designed to become active with only specific DNA."

"Why in the world did you create a virus like that?" Carmine asked.

Jamie ignored the question. "What we have is a virus that attacks the DNA of our greenhouses. Since we've found it, fixing this will not be difficult. The question is where did this virus come from?"

"Can you create a vaccine?"

"Yes, we'll begin that procedure by sending these micrographs to my lab. The equipment will quickly enhance the display. Once we determine the DNA of the virus, we can counter it. Failing that, we'll need to get them samples for analysis." He typed a code into the computer, and a tone sounded. "Okay, they've received it. Smiling, he took her arm, saying, "We might as well go to lunch."

***

Having first choice of the produce, the cafeteria at the greenhouse complex had great food. The salad was bursting with flavor, and the soup was a savory delight. "The food at Ocealla is spectacular but quite different from yours. This is mouthwatering. I had forgotten so many of the flavors you have here."

Carmine was confused. How could food be that different? She looked at Jamie. He stared back with an intensity that was not work related. Was she imagining an attraction? "Jamie, how is the sea rejuvenation project going?" she asked, brushing those thoughts out of her mind.

"After the Catastrophe, we rebuilt the food chain from the bottom up which meant creating algae that could live in the low light conditions on Earth. Once we had thriving colonies of algae, we introduced predators. Some were still around from before the Catastrophe, but we wanted ones that better fit the reproduction rate of our algae. The ones we designed liked to eat the wild predators too. At this point, we had an ecosystem on the micro scale."

As a young student, Carmine had written a paper about creating an ecosystem. Imagining the different species was fun. The genetic design was the difficult part.

Jamie continued, "From there we built up until we had food fish. Without the ability to inject designed species into the system, nature would take millennia to reach the same point we achieved. We would all be dead. It was a matter of survival."

Carmine's mind was awhirl. "This had to be started soon after the Catastrophe, and that was more than fifty years ago. You make it sound like you participated."

Whoops. She was too smart to fool with platitudes. "Perhaps I can tell you more soon but not now." Before she could respond, his phone sounded. Looking at the phone, Jamie frowned. "The actual samples need to be delivered to my lab."

Jamie through the Collective: [I need to get samples to the lab in Ocealla for analysis. The labs here don't have the capability.]

Kit: [Okay, I can arrange for you to send samples back.]

Jamie: [I need to go, and I'd like to take Carmine.]

Kit: [Whew! It's been a while since anyone other than Homakuwans were allowed in one of our cities. Jeremiah was the last. Why?]

Jamie: [I like her – a lot. I think she could be a valuable asset.]

Kit: [I think I understand. In all the decades I've known you, you have only been married to your work. What happened?]

Jamie: [I'm not sure. When I'm with her, and when I listen to her speak, it seems magical.]

Kit: [I trust your judgment. If you think she could become Homakuwan, I believe you. Do you believe that?]

Jamie: [I do.]

Chapter Twenty-Eight

With samples intact, the plane picked them up in Tucson, then headed for Hawaii. As the only passengers on the small electro-jet, they had the seats to themselves. "Sit back and relax. It's a long flight," said Jamie.

Carmine looked around the cabin. "This is the first time I've ever flown. I'm a little nervous."

"That's natural. Let me tell you a story about Ocealla which will take your mind off flying and fill you in on our destination. Long before the Catastrophe there was a small community near Baboquivari Peak. Do you know about it?"

Carmine smiled. "My grandfather told me the legends of the Tohono O'odham natives and how they believed that a new people, their people, emerged onto the Earth through Baboquivari Peak."

Jamie nodded. "That's the legend. This community called Kihhim was made up of scientists and engineers from the Biosphere 2 mission. Are you aware of this project?"

Carmine wrinkled her brow. "Something about a large greenhouse sealed from the outside world, an experiment that failed?"

"No experiment fails if something is learned," said Jamie. "You have parts of the story right. This group tried to create an ecosystem separate from Earth. It was a sealed greenhouse where everything was recycled and reused. Originally designed for six Biospherians, eight lived inside for two years. Oxygen levels and food production were low, resulting in painfully thin people when they emerged back onto the Earth's surface. Doubters and the press called it a failure, but it wasn't. After that project, our people believed we needed to live more in balance with our environment, so we started Kihhim. Kihhim is the Tohono O'odham word for 'the village' or 'the place I am from.' This community was underground, with large greenhouses supplying their food. It wasn't completely sealed off from the world, but meshed with it.

"To produce enough food to sustain the community, they used genetic techniques to enhance production, much the same as we are doing today. Their technology expanded, and they grew animals and even human body parts. As long as they remained hidden, nobody cared, but that didn't last."

Jamie frowned. "Once they were discovered, their technology was desired by governments and individuals. To keep from becoming prisoners, they fled and started an independent country at sea called Kahchk Kihhim. That means 'Sea Village' in Tohono O'odham. As a marine nation, they designed themselves for life at sea. They modified people to live underwater and enhanced dolphins' brains, making them citizens. It didn't stop there. In addition to the modified species, they created new ones, and in doing so became a new species on Earth. But it wasn't the creatures they created that were the new species, it was the creators who were new."

Jamie paused watching Carmine trying to process this idea. "To defend themselves, they extorted protection from the United States, but they knew that would not last. Humanity would not readily share the Earth with another intelligent native species. These descendants of humans at Kahchk Kihhim violated the biological definition of species, for physical characteristics did not define them. Understanding that their days were numbered, they designed a new species and a new habitat that could remain hidden from the surface world. They disappeared.

"The city they grew was called Ocealla, and that's where we are going. It is the capital of the nation of Homakuwa which has remained hidden for decades. Once it seemed that humanity was advanced enough to accept another species, Homakuwa emerged and joined the surface world to make a better Earth. They designed species to live in space and took over the Orbiting Power System and run it today."

The expression of wonder on Carmine's face told Jamie this was a new history to her. "When the Catastrophe occurred, they prevented total disaster on Earth using their genetic abilities. But their life-form designs were not limited to Earth. Homakuwa has spread out into the Solar system. We are going to the place where we design life."

Carmine was agog at this story. "So, who was the original Jamie Wong?"

"I am the only Jamie Wong. I created the organic computer that designs life through genetics and created the nation of Homakuwa. When the United States was the most powerful nation on Earth, I was alive. My computer designed the civilization now inhabiting the planets. I designed the greenhouses, I met your grandfather."

"But you look to be forty," cried Carmine. "You can't possibly be more than a century old!"

"More like two centuries. When you design life, you control aging. That's a simple thing."

The pilot came on the intercom and in a strange accent said they would be landing in a few minutes. Carmine froze. Jamie checked her seat belt.

As the stairway lowered, Jamie helped her off. It was night, and the warm humid air felt good. With her arm in his, he guided her to the side of the plane to retrieve their bags. She'd never seen a climate like this one and was overwhelmed, stunned into silence. With bags in hand, Jamie guided her to a waiting car.

Had he misjudged her? Was she unable to absorb this? If so, what a colossal mistake this had been. There was nothing to do but continue. The automated car stopped at an isolated stretch of beach. Jamie helped her out, and the car sped away.

Standing together on the beach, she looked around as if she were waking from a deep sleep. "Where are we?"

"We're on a beach in Maui. Our Traveler will be here soon. Do you want to sit down?" he asked gently.

"My legs are stiff from too much sitting. Let's walk a little." She looked at the surf racing up the sand. "This is really pretty. I've never seen the ocean. Will we be able to see it in Ocealla?"

"You will see more of the ocean than most people. I want to prepare you for the Traveler. It's…"

"There are more surprises?"

"Many more, but you must believe you are safe. The Traveler is a species designed to transport humanoids. Travelers are based on very large fish, bigger than whales. It's perfectly safe and will take us to Ocealla."

"It's an animal? Did you design it?"

"Yes, in a way. In Ocealla, we are a team—actually more than that. We are an organism with all of us as parts. Several worked on the Traveler design, and then we submitted it to the organic computer. It told us what needed to be done to make it a viable species." There was a loud splash. "Our ride has arrived," Jamie exclaimed, gesturing toward the surf.

As Carmine stared, a dark shape blotted out the small waves coming onto the beach. Before she could utter a word, Jamie picked up their bags and waded out, Carmine clinging to his arm. In front of them was an amorphous white hollow. As if he'd done it a million times, Jamie stepped up into it, reaching to guide her. Surprisingly soft underfoot, she and Jamie moved to the back. The minute they sat, the surface molded around them. A transparent film enclosed them in a bubble. Alarmed, Carmine clutched Jamie's arm as she watched the shore grow distant. They were moving out to sea.

***

The rhythmic back-and-forth sway of the Traveler was smooth as stars disappeared when they sank beneath the waves. The silence was interrupted only by the beating of her heart and the swishing of the water. Unsure of where they were going, she looked toward Jamie. Reading the concern in her eyes, he explained, "Don't worry, relax, sit back, and enjoy the ride. This trip is four hours. The Traveler will accommodate whatever you need. If you want to sleep, just think about it, and the Traveler will form a bed. If you need to use the facilities, think about it and they will form. This is a wonderful way to travel," he assured her.

She looked at him, worry in her eyes. "Give it a try. Think about taking a nap." The soft seat reclined to form a bed. The next thing she knew, Jamie was talking to her. "Carmine, time to wake up. Soon we'll be approaching Ocealla, and I want you to see it from the ocean."

She looked out at the dark water. "Here, put this on," Jamie said, holding out a white neck pillow. She placed it on her shoulders. The water brightened, and she could see outside. There were fish and other creatures swimming alongside the Traveler.

"What is this?" Carmine asked.

"It connects you with the Traveler so you are seeing through its eyes and senses. You're seeing electrical charges, light, heat, sound, and smell all put into your perception. When you learn to use these senses, you will perceive things miles away." The sea was alive around them. "Many of these creatures are citizens of Ocealla welcoming you. You are the first outsider to visit in more than four decades, and many of them have never seen a human. They are curious."

A dolphin-like creature swam close. Words formed in her mind. [Welcome. We look forward to meeting you.]

Carmine reacted in shock. Where did these words come from!

[I am Blue Streak, and I haven't met a human in a long time. We are so happy you have come to visit.]

Carmine whipped the collar off. "What is this thing?"

"It is a connector between you and the organism of Ocealla. When you wear it, you can speak with the citizens and with Ocealla itself. If you're uncomfortable wearing it, don't. It's okay."

The view outside was dark again. Gingerly, she put it back on. The sea brightened. Again words formed. [I am sorry if I startled you. We will remain silent until you are more accustomed to us.]

In the distance, a strange shape appeared. As the Traveler drew nearer, she could see a layer of glowing bubbles floating beneath the surface. Around it were hundreds of swimming shapes. The bubbles were huge–as large as a house. Inside, figures were waving at her. Tentatively, she waved in return but then pulled her hand back.

"It's okay," said Jamie. "They are greeting you."

The Traveler slowed as it neared, easing forward until it touched one and merged with it. The film dissolved. Jamie rose and took her hand. "Let's go inside. There are people I want you to meet." They stepped into the bubble. With a sucking sound, the Traveler withdrew, and the wall reformed. Carmine turned and watched it disappear, her only means of escape.

Chapter Twenty-Nine

A tall woman wearing a white robe approached. Holding out her hand, Carmine noticed her striking good looks, accented with green eyes and shoulder length blonde hair.

"I am Katharine Levey, president of Homakuwa, and I am pleased to meet you, Carmine."

Carmine took her hand automatically as if in a dream. Katharine Levey was a former president of the United World Government! What was she doing here? She looked around, observing several other people.

One-by-one, they approached her to introduce themselves, but the name that floored her was Ron Carson. This must be his great-great-grandson. The first Ron Carson was a name out of the history books. Not only was he a former president of the United States, but the first president of the United World Government. After the Catastrophe, he had been elected to lead the recovery team. This man looked fifty-years old. The first Ron Carson, the one in the history books, would be over two-hundred years old. She was stunned before realizing he was speaking to her.

"You are the first human to visit us several decades, and it is because Jamie Wong believes in you. Welcome."

"Thank you," she stuttered.

Katharine spoke, "I understand this has been a long trip for you, and it has been full of surprises. Do you need to rest for a while? It's past dinner time, Are you hungry?"

Carmine nodded. Katharine took her arm, leading her toward the wall. As they approached, it dissolved, and they entered another room. Carmine glanced back to see Ron and Jamie following. The opening closed behind them. A table formed from the floor, and chairs rose around it. Katharine walked her to a seat. Ron and Jamie joined them at the table.

"What would you like to eat?" asked Jamie. "We have good sea food."

Not able to believe what was happening, Carmine said nothing. "Let me get something for you," said Katharine. Silently, glasses of water rose from the surface of the table. Carmine drank from one, realizing how thirsty she was. A steaming bowl of thick soup rose as if from inside the table. Tentatively, she tasted it.

"This is delicious," Carmine said. "What's in it?"

Katharine smiled. "It's seafood chowder. Jamie tells us you are helping him solve the problems with the greenhouse disease."

Carmine found her voice. "Jamie is solving it. I'm here for the ride."

"And how are you finding the ride?" asked Ron.

"I am overawed. I never knew anything like this existed."

"Few people know of us. During your stay, you will learn why," said Katharine. "First, a little about the nation of Homakuwa is in order."

Carmine was rapt in the descriptions Katharine gave of the history of Homakuwa.

Katharine smiled. "Today we try to guide the human civilization so it will survive."

"When you say 'guide' what do you mean?" asked Carmine.

"See, I told you she was sharp," said Jamie.

Katharine continued, "With our technology, the recovery was accomplished in decades. Nature would take millennia and we'd all be extinct by then. The greenhouse project is a product of Jamie. Without that, starvation would have devastated humanity. We place people in offices of power to keep humanity thriving. Is it right or not? The bottom line is we live on this Earth too, and it is in our best interest that the world remains peaceful."

Carmine frowned. "You speak as if humanity cannot maintain itself."

Katharine smiled. "History illustrates that point, and we cannot gamble with our existence. Before the Catastrophe, we managed the fishing industry, which was on the verge of collapse from over-fishing. Under our direction, it thrived, and it will again. We continue to operate the Orbiting Power System which we've been doing from before the Catastrophe. We designed species to live in space." Katharine waved her hand over the table, and a holograph of one of the large collector mirrors appeared above it. The view closed on the collector, focusing on a single point that resolved itself into an access hatch. The view moved inside. A jellyfish-like creature moved within the cabin. It pulled itself with many arms, and jetted to another part of the cabin, like a balloon.

"This is one of our OPS operators who is so different from humanity she would never be accepted as an equal." The holograph changed to a view of Mars. "We spread out into the Solar system, and our first stop after the moon was Mars. Staging colonies on Deimos and Phobos have people more like a spider. Martian citizens are varied, but one of the most interesting resembles a tumbleweed."

A hologram of a skeleton of a ball consisting of green stalks without leaves appeared. As Carmine watched, it dried and became brown. A gust of wind started it rolling across the ground where it joined hundreds of others.

"Before the Catastrophe this Russian Thistle was common. With their light structure, the winds pushed them across the ground leaving a trail of seeds. Martians are very similar. Like a plant, they exist on carbon dioxide and light. They harvest light for energy, but as the wind rolls them around, they absorb additional energy from that motion. They don't have individual minds but are tied together in a common intelligence."

Carmine's gaze was intent as she studied this being—a totally alien creature created by the mind of Homakuwa.

"They are more plant than animal, so they exist on sunlight and wind energy. They, like all of our creations, are connected to the Collective mind."

Carmine's focus shifted to Katharine. "What's that?"

"When you put on the collar, it connects you with our Collective mind. On the Traveler, you were seeing the ocean through the Traveler's senses. It connected with you." Katharine held out a collar. "If you put this on, you can connect with us. You can speak with us and share our thoughts. You control what thoughts we see of yours, giving you privacy."

"Is this like the one on the Traveler?" Katharine nodded. Carmine reached for the collar and placed it around her neck.

"Close your eyes and let your mind go blank. Don't search, but just let it come," said Jamie.

Trying to form a blank in her mind, Carmine closed her eyes. At first, she saw only black, but soon dreamlike images formed. The first clear one was of her sitting in the chair wearing the collar. She was looking at herself through Jamie's eyes. A thought formed in her mind and she recognized it.

Jamie: [Just relax and let your mind expand. Let me take you on a tour outside of Ocealla. We're going to join with Blue Streak, the Dahlfin, who accompanied us when we were in the Traveler.] As if holding her hand, Jamie led her into another mind.

Blue Streak: [Welcome to the Collective. Let's go for a swim, so I can show you more of Ocealla.] Like a rocket, they sped past the bubble city. High above was the slivery mirror of the water surface. There were patches of green floating on it. They shot toward the surface and beyond, bursting into the air. [Those are the algae beds making oxygen for our air-breathing citizens. The algae beds also supply us with food.] They dove back into the depths. A squid-like creature swam past.

Blue Streak: [You met Unweil earlier.]

Her mind moved again, and a view of the sea in three-hundred degrees caused a wave of dizziness.

A new voice spoke.

Unweil: [I'm Unweil. We briefly met before. Don't try to focus what my eyes are seeing. Just relax and let me resolve it for you.] The dizziness went away, and she was a speck surrounded by the ocean. Input came to her from everywhere, and she was aware of everything around her.

Blue Streak: [We're just showing you Ocealla. Let's go visit Chetnaz. You'll really like her.]

Carmine's senses spun, and another mind coupled with hers. This one was sharp and crisp. She looked at the Earth as seen from a power satellite. Though much of it was covered by thin clouds, she saw patches of blue.

Chetnaz: [Hi, Carmine. I'm Chetnaz, one of our oldest space citizens. My job is the OPS, where we continue to beam energy to Earth, so I live here. If we look this way,] objects whizzed by, [we can see the moon.] A brilliant clear moon filled her view. [As with Unweil, I have sensors that can 'see' three-hundred and sixty degrees] This time, Carmine was floating in the vastness of space. The satellites, the Earth the moon, and the sun stretched out before her. She felt very small. [Don't let the size worry you. When you are with the Collective, you are as big as all of us together. That's larger than the Solar system. One of our newer members is farther away from Earth. See if you can tell where you are.]

Wispy clouds surrounded her but below the clouds thickened and swirled in currents like water. Above her, they thinned and a brilliant arch crossed the sky. She had never experienced anything like this scene. A moon raced across from one cloudy horizon to the other.

Sartay: [Hello, Carmine. I am Sartay. If you haven't guessed, I live on Saturn. That arch above us is the rings.]

Carmine: [How do you live here? I thought the gravity and the radiation were too great for life to exist.]

Sartay: [Both are too great for the type of life you are used to. I am a gas-filled membrane similar to Chetnaz in shape, though without the arms. I use the radiation energy from the planet to break methane into carbon and hydrogen. There's a lot of methane here. I form the carbon into nanotubes and weave them into the membrane that is my skin. The hydrogen is used to control my altitude. When I need to feed, I lower myself into the dense clouds and high radiation levels. Once I've had enough, I expand myself with the hydrogen and rise above the clouds.]

Carmine: [Where's your brain if you're all gas and carbon?]

Sartay: [Parts of my brain are within the carbon weaving, but it's not the brain of an individual you are talking to. We are connected to make one brain.]

A new vision of Saturn as seen from space appeared, but it was not the ringed gas giant in the history books. The fluid parts were there, but it was overlaid with a mesh that was the connection of the beings on the planet.

As she grew more comfortable, she allowed her mind to expand, noting the dimensions changing until the three she knew on Earth were only a small part of what she could fathom. Amazingly, she perceived the Solar system as a connected entity made up of the parts of every planet. Her brain started to hurt.

Jamie: [Time for you to go back. This can be tiring to those not accustomed to it.]

Suddenly, she was back in Ocealla, sitting in a chair, absolutely drained, her body was limp. Jamie lifted the collar from her. She said, "I'm not so much tired physically as I feel my mind is weary."

"That's the reaction I expected," said Katharine. "We'll let you rest and meet again tomorrow. Jamie will show you to your room."

At that, Jamie stood before her, offering his hand which she took, rising on unsteady legs. With effort, she placed one leg in front of the other. They moved toward the wall, and as an opening formed, passed through into another room. A bed formed out of the floor. A white wrap appeared on the wall.

"Make yourself at home. To wash up, just think of a bathroom, and one will form. You'll find the bed quite comfortable. After your journey, you need rest. I'll come for you in the morning." Jamie turned to leave.

As he was going through the wall, Carmine called after him, "Thank you, Jamie for bringing me here. It's wondrous."

Chapter Thirty

Not used to travel, Jamie went to his room tired. Once ready for bed, he lay down and joined Katharine, Ron, and Leticia in the Collective.

Jamie: [What do you think of her?]

Katharine: [I understand why you are attracted. She is very sharp and merged well in the Collective.]

Leticia: [It is your desire that she join us, and I see why. I think she would be a great asset, and perhaps a good companion for you. I'm for it.]

Ron: [What if she chooses not to join?]

Jamie: [I believe she will join or I wouldn't have asked her, but she has the option. In that case, we have to let her go.]

Leticia: [She could represent a danger to us.]

Jamie: [Carmine will realize it more over the next few days. She could choose not to join, but I don't believe she will be a danger to us once she knows why we are necessary to the well-being of humans.]

Katharine: [Rest, Jamie. We'll talk more in the morning.]

***

Carmine awoke from a dreamless sleep more refreshed than she had ever felt. A tone sounded and Jamie's voice spoke. "Will you be ready for breakfast in thirty minutes?"

Speaking to the wall, she said yes. Carmine looked around the featureless room. She thought of a bathroom, and one formed.

When she emerged from the shower, a towel hung nearby. A white one piece sheath hung from the wall. After she put it on, she wished for a mirror. Not surprised, one appeared before her. The white dress hung loosely. Idly, she pulled at the waist, and it tightened around her. She froze. What had just happened? Slowly Carmine pulled a sleeve, and it lengthened, the other changed to match. What had been a loose sheath was now an A-line. The fabric seemed to sense what she wanted. She thought of red, and the white changed into crimson. Carmine smiled. She could get to like this place a lot. As she put on the white shoes, they changed to match the dress. She spun in front of the mirror. Not too bad. A chime sounded. "Come in," she said. *Watch out, Jamie. I look good.*

Jamie entered and stopped, taking in her outfit. "You figured out our living fabrics. Good job!" Jamie was dressed in slacks and a casual shirt. "Are you ready for a hearty breakfast to prepare you for a hard day?"

"I am."

Guiding her through the opening into another small room, a table and two seats formed from the floor. "Let me order something for you."

Carmine laughed, "Since I don't know the menu, go ahead."

Without Jamie speaking, glasses of juice rose from the table. "This is a sea vegetable juice, but it tastes like tomato. We have eggs and bacon, if you'd like that."

"I've only heard about bacon. That hasn't been available since before the Catastrophe," she said. "We do have eggs, though."

Jamie laughed. "Oh, you'll like bacon. No pigs in Ocealla, but we can grow it in our vats. We can grow almost anything, so we have a good menu. We can even have steak for dinner, if you like."

"Steak! I've heard about that. It was the flesh of cows, right?"

"Ours isn't."

Fascinated, she watched the plates rise from the table loaded with scrambled eggs and strips of bacon. Picking up a piece, she turned it around before tasting. When the flavor hit her taste buds, her eyes grew wide. "Wow! So this is bacon. I could really learn to like this."

Jamie smiled. "You're not alone in that. We put the flavors in but remove the unhealthy parts."

After breakfast, they went to his lab. They stopped in a change room outside the lab door and went through the basic cleanroom procedures. The lab was a small room containing only a raised table.

"Okay, let's see what we've got." Jamie rubbed his hands together. From a compartment in the table, he removed one of the vials he had taken from the greenhouse and placed it on the table. A bubble formed over it, and a cloud formed inside. "We're sterilizing everything inside the bubble." The cloud cleared, and a tendril removed the cap from the vial. It reached inside, touched the sample, and withdrew. Another tendril closed the vial. The one with the sample froze, and the surface of the bubble became a microscope view.

"Here's our virus," Jamie pointed at the prickly spheroid shape. "Let's look at the DNA of this little beast." The view on the bubble formed dots and lines that scrolled downward. "Aha." Jamie pointed at the screen. "This sequence is what I want our greenhouse immune system to recognize. This will be the common sequence for a whole family of variations of this virus. Once the greenhouse sees this, its own antigens will consume the virus to protect itself."

A second screen appeared in the air above the bubble with a duplicate of the lines and dots in the first. "Okay, we'll remove this sequence," he said pointing at another area of lines and dots. "This will render it weak and allow the immune system of the greenhouse to recognize it and build antibodies." Some lines disappeared. "Okay, is this a viable species and will it make a good vaccine?"

The screen clouded over for a few seconds, and then the image returned. Part of it was in red. "Hmmm. It's not so easy. The sequence we removed weakened the virus too much, and it won't survive. Let's put it back." The lines and dots reappeared.

"Jamie, what are you doing?"

"I'm sorry. Let me explain. The upper screen here," he pointed, "is a design program tied to our organic computer, much like a brain. It creates a model based on the DNA we've created then checks viability of the species. What we want is a vaccine that educates the immune system so it recognizes this virus as a danger and triggers a response. It's the same as your immune system."

"I understand that. It's the computer simulation I'm asking about," said Carmine.

"When we first started genetic designs of life, we built a system to analyze the creations ensuring we did not create failures, or even worse monsters. The brain we grew analyzes our designs before creating a model to grow. Then it subjects the model to the conditions under which it must exist while checking variations the life form will take on in response to changes. In other words, it oversees our designs to prevent us from screwing up. We built the computer with the ability to grow and learn as well as guide our genetic work. When it sees a problem, we try to modify the design. Failing that, we abandon it. We never create a species until we understand what it will do."

Carmine looked around the room. "Where is this computer?"

"We call it the Architect Program, Architect for short. The physical part is throughout Ocealla and our other cities while the mental part is the Collective mind. We access it through the Collective. Would you like to experience it?"

Carmine hesitated. Jamie held out a collar. She looked at it. "Why don't you wear a collar?"

Jamie said, "Most of us have the role of the collar within us now."

She took and put it around her neck. "Okay, I guess."

"Close your eyes and let your mind go blank," Jamie said.

She did, and an image of Jamie formed. He moved toward her, and the image dissolved, but she felt his presence surround her.

Jamie: [At first, this will be disconcerting.]

Carmine: [It's all disconcerting. Let's go ahead.]

In pure darkness, Jamie's presence surrounded her like heat or an invisible cloud. She sensed she was expanding outward. A three-dimensional web formed, engulfing them. It seemed to be a nerve nexus–that was the only way to describe it. Flashes of light winked along pathways, and it pulsed. It was vast, but she could perceive any part she chose. Size meant nothing, time meant nothing.

Carmine: [Where are we, Jamie?]

Jamie: [We are in the Collective mind. It's not really a place as you think of a place. Yet, if you want, you can view any place through the eyes of anyone in the Collective mind. Would you like to experience Mars?]

The darkness around them was suddenly a dim red glow. Winds drove the dusty atmosphere against her, and she rolled across a sandy plain. The sky was black beyond the dust, and a moon was rising from the horizon.

Jamie: [Spread your mind out over the planet.]

Carmine relaxed and let her mind widen where she connected with more than the being rolling across the rocks and sand. She became the planet, and the wind, and the dust, and the sand, she was all of it, and it was conscious. It was sentient!

Carmine: [My God! I never knew.]

Jamie: [You had to have the Collective mind before you could understand. Our individual brains aren't large enough. There's more, and we keep exploring. Let's go back.]

Once again in Jamie's lab, Carmine blinked her eyes and looked around the room. "Jamie, this is so unbelievable. I'm not sure it's real."

"Of course, you're not. You will have to convince yourself, but you already know it is. Let's check on our vaccine."

The screen in the air above the bubble showed a new series of lines and dots. The changes were highlighted in blue. There weren't many. "I want to review what the Architect did." Another view appeared. This one was of cells actively moving on the screen. "These are immune system cells in the greenhouse. The Architect has installed them in the model of the greenhouse, and it has infected it with the virus."

They watched as the immune system cells actively sought out and devoured the virus-infected cells. "Okay, that part works," said Jamie. "Now the Architect will speed up time to check for adverse effects of the vaccine to the greenhouse. Each second of present time is a day in greenhouse time. That will accelerate until the Architect is satisfied there will be no further problems, even years into the future."

"Is this what you've used to design the ecosystem you built for the seas?" Carmine asked.

"Yes and what we're using for the land. Both systems are hugely more complicated than this one species test we've done. The interactions alone add exponential complications. That is why we needed a system as big as the Collective mind. The ecosystem of the Earth is limited by the environment and the time it takes to change. One thing we've learned is that nothing is static. The species we introduce also change as conditions change."

"It seems like our greenhouse operation is so small in comparison," said Carmine.

"Your greenhouse operation is key to human survival. It is not small. Without the food greenhouses produce, humans will perish."

"Why don't you combine with humanity?" she asked. "Why don't you offer the Collective?"

"It takes a very special person to enter the Collective mind. What you haven't experienced yet is the openness of letting the Collective into your mind. It means revealing your intimate self. Put the collar on again. I'll show you."

With the collar around her neck again, she closed her eyes. Jamie was with her.

Jamie: [This connection will be just you and me.] Jamie opened before her and invited her in. She was a part of Jamie, a part of his mind and knew everything about him. She began to explore his memories. She was back in Kihhim as he began to create human organs and grow them; as Jamie, she created sea creatures, gave them brain capacity and made them citizens of Kahchk Kihhim; as Jamie, she created the species that now inhabited space around Earth; and as Jamie she created a living spaceship.

Carmine understood the basic nature of Jamie, and she liked what she saw.

Carmine: [I want to go back now,] she said.

Carmine removed her collar and looked at Jamie. "I know you as I know myself. Did you enter me?"

"That would have to be by invitation when you're ready, but not until you choose. That is the openness that takes a special human, and not many are willing to share at that level."

"Why did you think I would?" Carmine asked.

"Over the centuries I have lived, I've learned to read people well. I may be wrong, but I think not." He smiled. "You get to choose soon, and as you already suspect, it will change your life forever."

"My life is already changed. What if I opt out of joining Homakuwa? What happens to me then?"

"Nothing. We go back to Tucson, which we will do anyway, and you continue your life as before."

"Aren't you afraid I'll reveal everything I've learned about Homakuwa?" she asked.

Jamie smiled. "You already understand that we are necessary to the existence of humanity. To harm us imperils the recovery of the Earth and harms them. You also understand that we are here to help, and there is nothing to be gained by revealing us to them. I sense that you want to be a part of us."

Carmine said nothing. Some things he said she hadn't even thought about herself, but as soon as he said them, she knew they were true. "You scare me, Jamie. You seem to know more about me than I do, and I didn't even invite you into my mind."

He looked into her eyes. "You've been inside mine. Is there anything to be scared of?" he asked.

"No. It's more of a sensation of being naked and vulnerable. I'm not used to that."

"Think of trust. Do you trust me?"

"I do," she said. "I trust you completely." Smiling, she continued, "Okay, I feel better now."

"The Architect has begun growing the vaccine for us to take back. It won't be ready for a day, so tomorrow we can tour and play. Consider it a day off. We can do whatever you want. I'll take you back to your room, so you can rest, and I'll pick you up for dinner. Some of our other citizens would like to join us. Is that agreeable?"

"I look forward to it." They exited the lab.

Chapter Thirty-One

Unable to rest because her mind whirled with what she'd learned, Carmine closed her eyes letting images from her experiences flow. Homakuwa was an advanced alien race, yet she saw humanity's roots pervading Jamie's mind. Although she looked forward to dinner, she was nervous about the future.

She would join Homakuwa because helping put Earth back together and rebuilding human civilization was a deep-seated part of her. Fascinated with the Collective mind and the experiences caused her to smile.

Then there was Jamie. She was drawn to him like a little girl imagining what love would be like. As an adult woman no man had caught her attention this way. Because she saw into his mind, she knew he could fall in love with her but was holding back, reserving that love until he knew what she wanted.

With this roiling in her mind, she tried one dress on, then another, tugging the living fabric here and there, changing it as her mind changed. Colors flowed like a rainbow. At last, she closed her eyes and let the emotions fly. When she opened them, she wore a red patterned flared skirt and a white peasant blouse in the old tradition of her father. It was perfect.

A tone sounded. "Enter." Jamie came in wearing a white robe, the uniform here.

Looking at this woman, he saw the aura surrounding her. Black hair coiled to her shoulders, framing her pretty face. The blouse and skirt gave hints of her slender figure. "I like the dress," he said. "You look fantastic."

"Thank you." She took his offered arm as they walked through the opening into another room. One wall of looked out into the unnaturally bright surrounding sea. Figures swam by, some the Dahlfin species, others the squid species, the Cons. In the background a Traveler approached.

As they entered, Katharine and Ron stood. Next to the table was a low-walled tank. A Dahlfin, a Con, and another figure floated. The third figure rose and stepped out. It was very tall, man-like with webbed hands and feet. Its dark skin glistened. "I am Sean Steel," the impressive creature said, holding out its huge webbed hand. "Welcome to Ocealla."

A bit unnerved, she responded, "Carmine Sanchez," as she watched her hand disappear in his. His skin was cold. A Traveler swam up to the wall and merged. A woman stepped into the room. Her skin was mocha colored, and she had short dark hair in tight coils. Catching Carmine's eyes with her own, she held them as she walked forward, hand extended.

"You must be Carmine Sanchez. I'm Leticia Gardner. A pleasure to meet you. I've learned so much about you," she said, glancing at Jamie Wong.

Carmine closed her gaping mouth, swallowed hard, answering in a weak voice, "I'm pleased to meet you." A jolt passed through her. This was the woman who was rebuilding her world! No taller than Carmine, she had an intimidating aura of confidence.

"It might be easier for us if you wore the collar, if you don't mind," said Jamie. "Many of our citizens want to meet you." Carmine put the collar on, thrilled to be a part of this group.

Blue Streak: [It is good to see you again. Jamie tells us you helped in the treatment of the greenhouse disease.]

Carmine: [Jamie and the Architect did everything. I just stood by and watched. It is fascinating.]

Unweil: [Isn't it though! It designed me and look how good I turned out.]

Leticia: [Jamie tells me you are considering joining us.]

Carmine: [I am. The trip I took through some of you into space and to Mars combined with the idea that you are dedicated to rescuing Earth and humanity captivated me.]

Katharine: [We are the progeny of humanity. Like children, we cannot let our parents go.]

A new mind entered the Collective with them.

Leticia: [I'd like to introduce you to Mohammad al Jar, the Prophet. This is Carmine.]

Warmth suffused through Carmine. The image of a man formed in her mind's eye. He wore the same white robe as the others, but his face was hidden within the folds of a cowl. She was stunned. Her father had raised her as a follower of the Prophet. She had watched him in holographic broadcasts, and more, she believed in him. Her mind froze.

The Prophet: [Welcome, Carmine.]

Carmine: [I... I didn't know you were part of Homakuwa.] She felt him laugh.

The Prophet: [You didn't even know about Homakuwa two days ago, so I understand.]

She laughed too. His presence drew apprehension from her. Suddenly this was the most wonderful thing that had ever happened. Joy bubbled around her buoying her up to an understanding that she belonged here.

***

Stepping into the Traveler, they waved goodbye to Ocealla. The huge fish slowly withdrew from the bubble, turned, and with a few sweeps of its giant tail, they moved away. Carmine was conscious of the Collective within so it wasn't as if she were leaving. Still, a new part of her had been born, and Ocealla was special.

Carmine: [Jamie, I'm ready to let you in.]

[Are you sure? Let me open to you first.]

She moved into his mind where she fit nicely. Carmine could read his thoughts: [I am a nice fit, aren't I?]

Their minds merged into one. Jamie felt her absorb him into herself. Her thoughts and memories were his, and his were hers. They marveled at the wonder of each other as they experienced the most possible intimate connection.

As her hand touched his shirt, Jamie sensed her hunger for him. The living fabric responded to her touch and melted away. He calmed her momentary embarrassment, he melted her sheath away. She glowed when he thought how beautiful she was.

She experienced his anticipation as she moved first one way and then another. His excitement was hers and hers was his. As she pulled him to her, she embraced him physically and mentally.

The movement of the Traveler was only one motion that moved them as they rose on an upward spiraling journey. In a nova-like explosion, they were engulfed in a detonation of pleasure that echoed between them. Each gave and received the sensations of the other. Slowly the waves subsided.

The rest of the trip passed much too quickly for them.

Chapter Thirty-Two

Jesus Zigarra and Leticia Gardner watched the endless field of grass move in the wind like swells on the ocean. The grass-covered plain stretched to the blue snow-capped mountains in the distance. In the years since the Dark had ended, scientific teams pushed the recovery of the Earth.

"Jesus, we've gotten the plains states moving well. We're a good team," said Leticia. "The genetically engineered grass thrives on the cool wet conditions of much of the world now."

"The windborne seeds our labs developed ensured that within a few years much of the land was covered. With the release of the herbivore species, the ecosystem is coming back. The seeds designed as a fine black powder were carried by the winds onto the ice sheets where they warmed and melted glaciers.

Jesus smiled. "As the snow and ice recedes northward, seasons are returning. The weather records say this is a cool summer for Arizona, but we're getting more days without clouds. It's time to begin the forestation program."

Pointing at the dark shaggy animals dotting the landscape and munching on the grass, Leticia noted, "That herd of buffazells has grown immensely without predators to control their population."

Homakuwa had designed the buffazells as an herbivore species with a fast reproduction rate, sending the embryos to labs and experimental farms. With multiple births each year, their numbers swelled to millions roaming the vast plains of the Americas and the other grasslands of the world.

They were small and slender, with a shaggy coat to protect them from the cold. Based on the sheep and goats of Earth before the Catastrophe, their short lifespan helped the species adapt to different climates as they migrated.

A cloud of sparrow-like birds swirled through the herd picking through the buffazells waste and distributing the grass seeds. High in the sky, larger birds circled above the herd.

"The egatures worked well in scavenging, but the buffazell herds have grown so fast they are overwhelmed," said Jesus. The egatures were a combination eagle and vulture, and helped process the carrion of the buffazells and the other small creatures.

Leticia nodded. "The coyenas will help with the scavenging. It's time to introduce them. Once the number of carcasses is reduced, both they and the egatures will become more of a predator species." The coyenas were a combination of hyena and coyote with tawny coats and powerful shoulders.

The buffazells would soon have to learn to cope with predators. Coyenas were pack animals with a slower reproduction rate. Leticia continued. "We've seen changes in the species. They're adapting as the climate warms and changes. They will survive. The prairie rodents have also thrived, and it's time to control their numbers. We'll introduce the weaselcats too."

"The diversification bodes well for us," said Jesus. "I had my doubts we could design species and grow them fast enough to meet the changes. Your idea of species with short lifespans and rapid reproduction rates is not only repopulating the fauna, but aiding in their adaptation to changing conditions. I'm beginning to believe we'll make a go of this."

Leticia nodded. "With the reforestation, we'll have other habitats, and the number of species will multiply exponentially. Soon, control will be out of our hands, and nature will take over. It's a gratifying feeling."

"We all deserve a pat on the back because we've accomplished in a century what would normally take millennia. My hat's off to you and the scientists in your labs," said Jesus.

PART 5

Chapter Thirty-Three

The robed man, known as the Prophet, stood before the crowd, arms raised. He was slender with a tan complexion and brown hair. An aura of peace emanated outward, filling the auditorium. The Prophet had a gift for touching the minds of those close to him and guiding them toward spiritual awareness.

A child approached holding out a package wrapped in bright blue paper. Smiling, he looked down, reaching for the package. When his hand touched it, the world disappeared in a blinding flash and deafening roar. He never felt the concussion or saw the circle of blasted body parts. Screaming in panic, the crowd fled through the door of the auditorium, only to face a large banner hung from the opposite wall. "Spawn of the Devil-Child of the Un-natural. Destroyer of millions!"

***

Kit: [It's been nearly two-hundred years since a religious attack took place! What happened? Who did this?] Kit was in his first term as president of the United World Government.

Ron Carson: ['Outlanders for Humanity' is the name of the organization claiming responsibility. The manifesto published online today claimed the Prophet was the enemy of humans, responsible for the death of masses of humanity. They claim the Prophet led millions into the arenas where they died.]

Kit: [Unfortunately, that's true. But we all understand it had to be done. It happened so long ago, who's remembering that?]

Ron: [The leader of Outlanders for humanity is the great-grandson of Jacob. He was the assistant to Jeremiah, the Outlander who joined Homakuwa. Jeremiah now oversees the Southwestern District of the old United States.]

Leticia: [Jeremiah, are you with us?]

Jeremiah: [I'm here, and I'm shocked at what's happened. Jacob was loyal and believed in the Outlander society. An incident in his past comes to mind and may have fostered this. He and I were watching as the Prophet led thousands of people into the arena in Phoenix. Jacob's wife was in that crowd.

I had to hold him back to keep him from trying to save her. I thought he had moved past that, but obviously, he told the story to his children and grandchildren.

[Jacob always wanted the Outland society to get better recognition for their contribution to the recovery of humans. It's possible that his great-grandchildren took that up as a cause.]

Leticia: [The question before us is what to do about it now. Do we send out security forces? We must respond.]

Kit: [They've put forth no demands. We don't even know what they want. Is their purpose to kill the Prophet?]

Ron: [That won't happen. As in the years of religious unrest, another Prophet is already addressing crowds of people. We haven't had to bring in any of our clones in decades, but obviously humans are not past those actions.]

Leticia: [Then we will have another attack.]

The Prophet: [I am an integral part of UWG society. This is an attack on the UWG disguised as an attack on me.]

Jeremiah: [I agree. This is an uprising of the Outland society. Can we pinpoint the location of this group?]

Leticia: [Let's find them, shut off their power, and isolate them. What are they doing for food? What greenhouses are they using? We need information, so we know what to do about them.]

Chapter Thirty-Four

Jeremiah calmed those surrounding him as Kit's face appeared in the monitor. "President Carson, the group who's investigating the attack by the Outlanders is here, and we need to bring you up to date. Beside me is Tucson Police Chief Maria Ronstadt who is leading this investigation."

A dark-complexioned, short woman with black curly hair stepped into view. "We tapped every resource we could from the area of what used to be Arizona. Here's what we've found.

"The Outlanders for humanity includes not only some of Outlander society, but also the Wild-ones in Gila Bend. We're not sure of their total numbers, but our best estimate is three-hundred hard core members and an equal number of fence sitters. They are not a large group. They headquarter in Wintersburg, Arizona, an isolated community fifty miles west of Phoenix and the site of the old Palo Verde nuclear plant."

A hologram of the nuclear power plant appeared. "We sent in a drone. It shows greenhouses, but also, they are cultivating the surrounding land. If they get the power plant operating, we could not use power from the OPS as a lever against them."

"What are the chances of that?" asked Kit.

"There are no records of what was left there when Palo Verde shut down," said Chief Ronstadt. "All records were lost after the Catastrophe. It's possible there are enough fuel rods in storage to start it up at reduced capacity. We don't know what technical ability they have."

"Jeremiah, what does your team recommend we do?" asked Kit.

"Mr. President, at this stage, our consensus is that we try to bottle them up and isolate Wintersburg. They almost certainly infiltrated other areas of the Outland community, but we don't know how radical other members are. Turn off the OPS feeds to the area and force them to work at getting power themselves. They may not have the ability to start up the plant. The fly in that ointment is that there are a lot of solar cells on the rooftops of the buildings, and there is now enough sunlight to make power."

"That sounds like the plan for now. We'll shut off the Orbiting Power feed and see what their next move is. In the meantime, let's block all egress from Wintersburg and Gila Bend and isolate them," said Katharine. People surrounding Jeremiah nodded their agreement.

Jeremiah held up his hand. "Please wait, Mr. President. Pima County Sheriff Burger has something to add."

Stepping forward, the sheriff explained, "We're treating this as an isolated event, but are looking for members of a religious sect to question. The church is located in a small community south of Tucson along the Santa Cruz River, one of the few above-ground towns in this area. Originally, these people were with us here in Tucson, but when Roberto Espinoza Galvez started a church, the trouble began. Claiming he is a preacher, his radicalization became a threat, so two years ago we kicked them out. They headed south where they found an abandoned church and vacant homes at the deserted town of Tubac." A hologram map showed the area.

"Their farming efforts failed. The only thing between them and starvation are handouts we give them from our stores in Tucson. We reckon the preacher and his followers joined this campaign to take their minds off their empty bellies. We're watching him and his group to see if they have any ties to the Outlanders for humanity."

"Thank you, Sheriff. How many casualties were there?" asked Kit.

"So far, we've got five bodies, including the Prophet, twenty-three injured, three missing and we're still cleaning up the mess. I've got officers in Tubac with warrants looking for Roberto now. Not a lot of places he can hide, so we'll get him."

"Chief Ronstadt, what's the mood in Tucson?"

"Most of the people are still in shock. There was resentment before, but now they are furious at Roberto."

"And the attitude toward Outlanders?" asked Kit.

"Their involvement is not well publicized, so they won't harbor good feeling toward the Outlanders," said the chief. "Many here have concerns because a lot of our people, especially the youth went into the Outland to work with the salvage and Mech factories under the incentive programs we put in place. Is there any danger facing them?"

"Not that we've seen," said Kit. "The attacks are on the UWG warehouses, but not on the Outland salvage communities."

"Keep a watch for us, will you?" asked the chief.

Chapter Thirty-Five

The explosion rocked the assembly hall, dust flew, and a light crashed from the ceiling as people dove under tables. Another explosion shook the floor under them. UWG president, Kit Carson, was holding a meeting with the agricultural leaders for the United World Government to discuss the expansion into land available since the glaciers had retreated. Human civilization was on the verge of recovering. The skies were clear after two-hundred years, and the temperatures rising. It had taken two centuries to reestablish the ecology on the Earth's surface.

President Kit Carson had been in office for six years after two terms as the governor of the Southwestern Region of the United States. Kit connected with Homakuwa's Collective mind for information.

Kit: [What's going on?]

His wife Leticia Gardener answered. [Someone attacked the city. We're working to find out who. The attack was stopped but we don't know who is responsible for that either.]

Kit: [Get back to me as soon as you have more information.] With a deep sigh, he focused his attention to the chaotic meeting hall. People continued to scream. At the microphone, he yelled "Quiet." The room grew silent. "The attack on the city has halted. Let's exit in an orderly fashion. When I receive more information, you will be advised of another meeting. Please return to the safety of your homes until the announcement. That is all I have at this time."

A roar of questions erupted, but Kit ignored them, went to his office where he once again entered the Collective mind. [Okay, what do we know?]

Leticia: [The Mechs attacked.]

Kit: [The Mechs! We had an agreement with them. What happened?]

Leticia: [One of the AI's took control of a Mech salvage team and attacked. We think it's a conflict within the Mech civilization.]

Kit: [Set up a meeting with Prime. We have to get this straightened out. What stopped the attack?]

Leticia: [Another group of Mechs. Obviously, this doesn't involve all Mechs.]

Kit: [Was anybody hurt in the attack?]

Leticia: [A food warehouse was emptied and then destroyed, but no humans were inside.]

Kit: [Thank goodness for that.]

Jeremiah: [Interesting that the warehouse was emptied.]

Chapter Thirty-Six

The members of President Kit Carson's team investigating the Mech attack met in the conference room. The police officials for the City of Tucson, Pima County and Arizona were there, along with Governor Jeremiah Clark. A speaker broadcast AI Prime's voice. In addition, Homakuwa listened through the Collective.

Kit opened the meeting. "I want to thank you for attending today. The issue is the Mech attack last week. Jeremiah, could you give us a quick review."

"One of our food warehouses was attacked by a force of salvage Mechs . The attack was stopped by the warehouse Mechs. What is significant is that the warehouse was looted. Mechs don't need food, so why did they take it?"

"Prime, what did you find out?" asked Kit.

Prime's simulated voice spoke. "Mr. President, the AI controlling an idle team of Mechs was in

Phoenix. A virus invaded the AI that allowed for outside control."

"What do you mean by outside control?" asked Leticia.

"Human control," said Prime. "I've traced the virus to a computer in Wintersburg, Arizona. The instructions to attack were relayed there from Gila Bend. It was a human operation."

"That would explain the looting of food," said Jeremiah. "What do we do about it?"

"Prime, can you block the virus?" asked Kit.

"The virus has been isolated, but the opening for others exists. I can go in through a backdoor we programmed into the hardware, but it has to be a onetime change, because it will reveal the entry."

"We should attack them," said Tucson Police Chief Ronstadt. "We can mount a raid of the area within a day or two."

"Let's think this through," said Jeremiah. "A raid won't be enough. We'll have to kill or capture them all, and we must hit Gila Bend and Wintersburg simultaneously. Gila Bend is wide open, and a soft target. Wintersburg, as a nuclear power plant, has security measures we would have a hard time overcoming." He looked at the group. "What do we do with captives?"

Kit asked, "Don't you think we could hit them hard enough to convince them to stay away?"

"As an ex-Outlander, it wouldn't work for me," said Jeremiah. "The hatred of being abandoned and left to die, of seeing the Angel of Death in the form of the Prophet lure your loved ones away, of being always second-class citizens is too deeply ingrained. It has been passed down through the generations with the Prophet being the bogeyman to frighten children."

"Let's close this meeting and think on this for a while," said Kit. "Prime, thank you for your information. Can you prevent further kidnapping of Mechs?"

"Antivirus programs are installed, but within the hardware remains an opening for them. Takeover attempts can be halted on a temporary basis."

"Ladies and gentleman, I will notify you of another meeting, In the meantime, stay watchful and gather all the information you can. Thank you for your time."

***

Katharine: [Jeremiah, a lot of Homakuwa has been in on this meeting. Do you believe the Wild-ones and the rogue Outlanders cannot live peacefully with the UWG?]

Jeremiah: [Humans came from a 'survival of the fittest' evolution. It is in their basic DNA to seek status, dominate competitors, overcome opposition, and survive at all costs. Violence is in their nature. These people are human with all that entails.]

Katharine: [Does that make us the same if our only solution is to wipe them out?]

Jeremiah: [Vying for resources is their inheritance, not yours, but in trying to ally with them, you are riding the same train.]

Ron: [I've been in on this, and what I'm hearing is that Homakuwa should consider pulling out of the human world and leave them to their own devices. They will survive, or not.]

Jeremiah: [That does seem to be where this is going. For myself, I won't pull out. I'll go to Wintersburg to observe the situation. It's possible that these Outlanders are a culture of raiders and pillagers that will not change for the next few generations. In human history, there were many cultures like that. They were the predators of the human world. The Earth was more primitive then, but we're not far from that now.]

Leticia: [Civilization is a thin veneer that can be scratched away and beneath lies the raw nature. We steered humanity away from the disaster of the

Catastrophe and the brink of extinction, and we will soon have the Earth back on an ecosystem that will sustain animal life.]

Jamie: [If we walk away, humanity will survive. Frankly, my thoughts are turning back to Kihhim. I'm going to take a little trip there and see what it would take to revive it. Maybe I'm hearing my own persona and more than two-hundred years of life talking, but I'm tired. I'm taking a vacation.]

Carmine: [I'll join you. I've never seen Kihhim except through your memories.]

Jamie: [Don should be with us, too.]

Don: [I will be there.]

Katharine: [Ron, you've never seen Kihhim. Want to join me there?]

Ron: [Yes, I'd like to. Kit, how about you and Leticia?]

Leticia: [We're in! Let's have a reunion there. Carol, Dayton, are you game?]

Dayton: [We are.]

Rich: [I'll leave China today and pick up John from South America on the way. He's never seen it either.]

Rich: [Jeremiah, do you want to see where it all started?]

Jeremiah: [I do. We can meet in Tucson in two days. I'll get vehicles for the drive.]

Rich: [John and I will fly into Ryan Field, so you can get us on the way.]

Chapter Thirty-Seven

The Ajo highway was a main road to the port of Puerto Peñasco, so it was maintained well by a team of Mechs. Prairie grass sometimes higher than the cab of the Humvees covered the landscape. At the old junction of Three Points, they turned south. Since it was not maintained, the road had degenerated into little more than a trail.

Katharine: [It looks primordial. Leticia, Jamie, you've done wonderful things to bring life back. The last images I saw were of charred and barren ground.]

Leticia: [Jamie did the designs.]

Carmine: [How long did this trip take when Kihhim was inhabited?]

Carol: [From Tucson to the Kihhim gate was less than an hour. It was close enough to be convenient but far enough away to keep us isolated. Kihhim was also only thirty minutes from the Mexican border. When we fled the United States, we used that crossing for the three-hour trip to Puerto Peñasco on the coast.]

They quietly explored memories of Kihhim through the Collective. When Leticia turned west off the trail, no road was clear. Grass higher than the hood obscured any view.

Katharine: [Leticia, how can you see where we're going?]

Leticia: [Take a look.]

Looking through Leticia, Katharine saw a satellite view of themselves plowing through the grass like an icebreaker through solid floes of ice.

Chetnaz: [How do you like this view, Katharine? I'm using a radar map overlaid with this optical view to find the trail.] A faint broken line crossed the hill. [Visually, the trail is covered, but the radar is able to pick it up.] The line ended in a valley as they entered.

Leticia: [We're here!]

When they climbed out of the Humvees they stretched to get the kinks out after hours of being thrown around the inside. Lush with grass, the hill in front of them had a large cavern-like opening. To the side were frameworks, but the glass of the greenhouses was gone. A composite view of Kihhim formed in the Collective, with each former resident adding detail from their memory. Kihhim, the birthplace of Homakuwa was a ghostly overlay atop the ruin in front of them.

Katharine: [Let's go in.]

Ron: [Be cautious. It doesn't look stable.]

Carol: [The underground garage has held up well.] The cavern was empty and dark. She flashed her light around as layers of dust puffed at each step. [This way.] Carol led them to a door. When she pushed on the metal surface, it creaked open.

Rich: [Well, the glass of the atrium held up.]

High above them light filtered through the grimy panes, offering a dim view inside. As their eyes adjusted, the view changed to an open space, images of a cascading waterfall and hanging plants rose from the past. They split up, each going to the areas that were most familiar.

Jamie and Don looked through the door at the dusty tiers within the greenhouse structure.

Jamie: [It wouldn't be too hard to restart this. I could grow new greenhouses instead of the constructed ones we had.]

Don: [We still have most of the zygotes to start the growing, so that would be quick. I could have one greenhouse producing within three months after you got the greenhouse structured.]

Rich: [The well looks good. Jamie, can you design a biologic pump to replace the mechanical one?]

Jamie: [Sure. It'll be like the system we use to pump air downward from the algae fields at Ocealla along with tubes of muscle tissue with peristaltic pumping.]

Rich: [I can get photo-panels moved out here to give us electricity, and Chetnaz can direct power so we have it producing twenty-four hours.]

Jeremiah: [I can understand this being the birthplace. We've come so far, but the basics are here: underground housing, greenhouses, biological technology, solar energy. I'll bet everything was recycled.]

Jamie: [It was. We weren't fully isolated, like the Biosphere 2 project, but we were close. In the vernacular of the old era, we had a very small footprint.]

Katharine: [Jamie, what are you going to do here?]

Jamie: [I'm going to start it up. I'll get it rebuilt and growing.]

Katharine: [And after that?]

Jamie: [I'm not sure. This may be my last project. It may be time to go into the Collective.]

Carmine: [Oh, Jamie, this isn't a total surprise, and I've seen it within you. But hearing you say it makes it real, and it hurts me.]

Jamie: [Too early to say. Things change.] The Collective was silent.

In the valley, the setting sun moved the shadow of Baboquivari Peak until it touched the entrance to the underground community. After a last golden glint, dusk settled in.

Chapter Thirty-Eight

Jeremiah walked down the dusty path toward the gate to the old Palo Verde nuclear plant. When it had been operating at full capacity, it was one of the largest electric generators in the United States. After the Orbiting Power System was fully on line, it had been mothballed. A tall heavy man stepped out of the gatehouse, an assault rifle slung across his shoulders. The buttons on his black shirt strained to stay closed over his large frame.

"Whaddya want?"

"I want to join," said Jeremiah.

"Where ya from?"

"Phoenix," answered Jeremiah.

"How'd ya get here?"

"Walked."

The guard's eyebrows rose. "Wait over there." He pointed to a bench.

While Jeremiah waited, he thought. This was a dangerous step, but one he had to take. Would they believe he had walked all the way from Phoenix? Rich had dropped him off on the old US 80 Highway. As he walked, he saw a lot of traditional farming. With sunshine, the rainy climate, and cooler temperatures, it was easy to grow crops. These people didn't need the high tech greenhouses. A dilapidated electric Toyota drove up. The man who stepped out had all the features of his great-grandfather, Jacob, except he was smaller with thin hair and a weasely face. He strode over to Jeremiah.

"Who are you?"

"My name is Jeremiah Clark. Who are you?"

"I'm Lucas. Jeremiah, huh? Name sounds familiar. Do I know you?"

"We've never met."

"So you're from Phoenix?"

"I've been there and other places," said Jeremiah.

"What are you doing here?"

"I worked with the salvage teams for a while. Before that, I survived, doing whatever it took."

"Yeah, I hear that. We all did. Why you leave the salvage team?"

"There were things about the UWG I just didn't like."

"Yeah? Like what?" Lucas's eyes narrowed.

"I didn't like the way they treated Outlanders, and I especially didn't like the way they treated Wild-ones," confessed Jeremiah truthfully.

"What skills you got?"

"I'm good at organizing and getting things done."

"Har har. That's my job."

"Need help?"

Again Lucas' eyes narrowed. He rubbed his chin. "Yea, maybe. You know anything about computers?"

"I know how to use them," answered Jeremiah.

"Okay, we'll give you a trial run. Git in." Lucas gestured at the car.

They bumped over the cracked concrete road. "I saw a lot of farming walking here. Is that your group?"

"Ha, My group! I don't have a group. Like you, we didn't like the UWG so we came out here and started our own town. Since we can feed ourselves without their greenhouses, we don't need them."

"What about the Mech labor? Don't tell me all of this is done by people."

"Yeah, most of it is. We do have Mechs to repair our equipment an' stuff. You know, they got good records on stuff. We got kids who are whizzes with

Mechs, too. More people from the UWG keep coming to join. Our tractors are old, but we keep 'em working."

The monstrous cooling towers rose before them. "Your headquarters is in there?" asked Jeremiah, pointing.

"Some of the guys are worried about an attack by the UWG. It's safe in there."

"Why would the UWG care about you?"

"We been raisin' a little chaos with them. Some of the food and seeds we don't have, so we take 'em. Been getting a few more Mechs, too. We do like to target the protein tanks. Stuff is good, tastes like meat I'm told. I never tasted beef or pork. We got chickens and rabbits, but that's about it," said Lucas.

"Stealing from them seems like poking the tiger," said Jeremiah.

"Yeah, but we don't take much. Try not to be enough bother to rile 'em."

"You attack them yourselves?"

"Nah, we reprogrammed an AI, and it controls some Mechs to actually go in. But we know they'll figure out what happened and blame us."

"What will you do then?" asked Jeremiah.

"Fight, I guess. We've been working on the AI to wage a control war if they use Mechs against us. It can block their control signals and take over. We been making some weapons, but in a fight with UWG security, we'd lose. Our only hope would be to stock up the containment building and stay in there."

"How's the farming going? What are you raising?"

"We got fruits and veggies, and some fields of oats and wheat are coming along. Cotton's growing, too. We could do alfalfa but we don't have any animals. Nobody does, and the plains herds are too far away for us."

Jeremiah: [What if we got them pig and cow embryos. Could you do that, Jamie?]

Jamie: [We have everything, and I can tweak them a bit to grow faster. Yes, the answer is.]

"Lucas, before the Catastrophe, a lot of embryos were stored, and I know where. What if I were to get you pigs and cows? If you raised enough, you'd have trading materials for the UWG and wouldn't need to steal."

"You think you could get those?" a tone of wonder in Lucas' voice. "Where are they?"

"There was an underground storage lab on the campus of Arizona State University in Tempe. If the power wasn't cut off, they should still be good."

"What do you need? How many guys?"

"Let me think it through, and I'll get you a plan."

***

Jeremiah: [We can support the Outlanders by providing livestock. They aren't dependent on greenhouses. Bringing them livestock will strengthen my status.]

Kit: [You think you could move into a position of influence with them?]

Jeremiah: [Yeah and that could be a way of getting control over the conflict. The other thing that would help is getting them Mech help with their agricultural equipment. I don't propose that we use the Mechs in agriculture, but to refurbish their old equipment. They have a strong desire to be 'hands on' rather than depend on Mechs. There's a lot of stuff around, but it needs rebuilding.]

Carmine: [You want to support them? Since I've taken over the Arizona sector, we've been attacked six times. To date there have been no human casualties but the first time there are, the clamor to attack the Outlanders will be hard to quell.]

Katharine: [If we can defuse the reason for the attacks, they should stop. Jeremiah, how open is Lucas to stopping the attacks?]

Jeremiah: [Lucas is anxious to get the livestock program going, but he has an agenda outside of that. He hates the UWG. Even with livestock to trade and little economic reason to attack, he will.]

Leticia: [What about his followers? Do they feel the same way?]

Jeremiah: [If it came to a vote, he would get enough support. His people are made up of unhappy Outlanders. There are older people and youths who are passionate about independence. There's also a guy named Espinosa who preaches old-style gospel. With a small group from the south, he's trying to create a conflict with the Prophet and Faithism.]

Ron: [Can you erode some of that support and take over?]

Jeremiah: [Given time, and success with the livestock program, probably. This is a thriving community with babies being born. His group holds the seeds of a new society, and the vitality is because of their independence, the opportunity to profit from individual labor, and the conflict with the UWG. I don't want to tame them down too much, just keep them from being wiped out by strength of numbers. I do want to keep Espinosa and his religion out of control.]

Leticia: [Let's set up another meeting with Prime. Perhaps what we need is a Mech on Mech conflict with few human casualties.]

Rich: [Prime should get something for this program.]

Chetnaz: [Prime wants assistance in getting Mechs off Earth. Is a joint Homakuwa-Mech society possible?]

Leticia: [Perhaps it's time for that.]

Chapter Thirty-Nine

Mechs crawled over the exterior of the large meteoroid like ants on a log. Behind them a blue planet serenely spun. The space rock had been formed into the cylindrical shape of the Homakuwa habitats, and the large mirror used to heat and shape it was now powering a foundry. This factory would manufacture more Mechs and be the home base for the Mech society in space.

"Prime, what do you think about the new base?" asked Chetnaz.

"The thick walls of the meteoroid structure will protect our chip manufacturing from radiation. Thank you for the focusing mirror. If we had to build one, it would take a year. The radio equipment we lifted to orbit is functioning well, giving clear transmissions. Tomorrow, an AI will be on board to take control of the fabrication of the Mech space colony."

Leticia broke in. "Prime, how is the conflict program going?"

"The Outlander Mechs attacked a Tucson warehouse and destroyed three UWG Mechs. One Outlander Mech was lost. The factory in Las Vegas will be able to make up for the loss. A similar attack took place in Silicon Valley, but the chip manufacturers are safe. The second manufacturing factory in orbit will be a welcome security measure. Letitia, Mechs do not to attack the chip manufacturers. With humans starting to take part, those sites are in danger. To what extent do we protect the chip factories?"

"Prime, we are trying to avoid humans versus Mech fighting. We'll talk this over and schedule another meeting."

PART 6

Chapter Forty

The Milky Way galaxy filled Sylvix's view. The density of star systems blotted out the background of space, but the center abruptly became a circle of total black. The glow of gravity waves intensified into a glare in colors that the human eye could never see.

Sylvix: [Leticia, are you seeing this? It's the brightest and sharpest view ever.]

Leticia: [Yes, the vastness emphasizes how small we are. Most of those stars have planets orbiting them plus the giant black hole in the middle!]

Most humans would have found Sylvix's trip toward the center of the galaxy boring and deadly. The radiation intensity had increased to fatal levels to humans. She'd left the Solar system over two-hundred years ago. Like the other starships, she had picked up speed through each star system she'd encountered and was now hurtling forward at 0.5 light speed. As with the rest of the starships, the voyage changed her.

Space was not great emptiness with intermittent star systems. It pulsed with energy and the building blocks of matter. Ahead, a bright glow of gravity waves from a star system drew her attention. Since her departure from the Solar system, she had encountered many such systems. This one had brighter gravity waves than most but contained the usual mottled halo that surrounded a star system with planets. Perhaps it was a binary system though it shone brighter than just a star.

In the more than three-hundred years since the Homakuwa species was born, they had grown and changed. They began as humans with a special technology, hiding under the sea. Genetically variable in design, they grew into space and expanded beyond the Sol star system.

All these starships were organic entities within themselves. Some were colonies–space nomads containing many beings–while others were solo starships. Sylvix was an organism, a starship grown with the purpose of expanding Homakuwa and the Collective mind and learning about the universe. Sylvix was the first spaceship grown by Homakuwa, using genetics as humans used tools to create what they needed. She <u>was</u> the starship. More than two centuries before, she left the Sol star system with the goal of reaching the center of the Milky Way galaxy. Time measured in years had ceased to have meaning. Like Homakuwa, she could regenerate herself indefinitely–she was immortal. Starting as a space-species, they built enhanced abilities as they moved through the universe.

Though her physical self was the starship, her mind was part of the Homakuwa Collective. As her species grew throughout their home star system, their Collective mind allowed them to be part of a whole being that now made up the system of the star Sol. It consisted of more than the sum of the individuals.

Chapter Forty-One

Leticia: [Ron, Katharine, anybody, the crux is if the humans attack the chip manufacturers, we may not be able to make more Mechs. If the Mechs defend against a human attack, we will have Mechs battling humans.]

Katharine: [That sounds like more conflict than we want.]

Jeremiah: [It is inevitable, whether it happens now or in ten years. The Mechs are another native intelligent species with a right to share in living on Earth, just as Homakuwa does.]

Ron: [At least some humans will disagree with that. We've arrived at a decision point. As much as I hate to say it, humans must have conflict to survive. How much longer do we try to prevent their demise, either from outside forces or from themselves?]

Leticia: [Are you saying that we leave Earth?]

Kit: [What about us Homakuwans here on Earth? We're mostly human with the same inability to exist elsewhere.]

Ron: [We are in the Collective. We can continue there. What I'm saying is maybe it's time to quit trying to steer humanity.]

Katharine: [What will we do? As much as I love Ocealla, I also like the surface world, and I'm not willing to hide under the seas.]

Ron: [I'm saying we continue trying to guide, but the fate of humanity lies with them. What we can do is prevent them from destroying us in their continued conflicts. I no longer have a moral objection to changing humanity when necessary.]

Leticia: [Using this concern about the chip manufacturing plants, what are you suggesting?]

Ron: [We need to bring AI Prime into this discussion, but I think we should build chip plants underground and hidden from humans. We already started with the orbiting ones.]

Kit: [When they attack the plant and destroy the ability to make more Mechs from it, do we let them do without Mechs?]

Ron: [That will be my suggestion to Prime. Let the Mechs start a separate nation. Mechs have one in

Korea, another in Antarctica, and others in zones not easily habitable by humans.]

Leticia: [Prime can transfer to orbiting entities leaving behind a part of the Mech civilization.]

Katharine: [War between the Earth-side Mechs and the humans may pull us in, if the humans know enough about us. They will consider biologic life allies in opposing Mechanicals because they cannot conceive Mechanicals as a form of life.]

Leticia: [When our civilization was formed, we did what was necessary to survive. Neither our existence nor the Mechs' existence on Earth is critical to our survival any longer. Both of our civilizations are spreading well beyond Earth.]

Sylvix: [Leticia and I remain close, but when I try to show her other dimensions and other senses that have developed within us, she cannot see them. We are seeing changes in ourselves as we move farther into the Universe. Our Collective mind has become greater than that of the Collective mind of the star system of Sol. Much of it you cannot perceive, and we are not sure why. We believe that to evolve, we must spread out through the Universe. As great as the entity of Sol is, there is much more.]

The Prophet: [Centuries ago, when the Catastrophe happened, humanity was headed for extinction, and the Earth was poised to remake itself. New species would rise and evolve. A new line of progression would take place–a new flow of evolution would begin. Homakuwa's intervention did not change this progression, but it did change the timeframe, and in the scope of the Universe, time is meaningless. Humanity has served its purpose, giving birth to you. Humans will survive until the next calamity.]

Katharine: [What about the Mechs? Humanity created them, and it's another civilization.]

The Prophet: [Mechs are another civilization, but it can never progress past the physical universe. It will grow and spread throughout the universe, but due to the laws of physics under which they exist, time and distance limits them. You are on a path that leads beyond the physical universe. The Universe is so much more than the physical you know from Earth. Sylvix and the star Homakuwa civilization are beginning to see that. They are the next step in evolution, and you gave birth to them.]

Leticia: [So, just as humans gave birth to us, creating a descendant species, we will be left behind by our descendant species.]

The Prophet: [You must examine the term 'left behind.' No one is 'left behind.' The evolution river does not carry species forward. It generates new species that move forward. The flow of evolution is more like an ocean wave. The wave moves forward, but the individual particles do not. When Kihhim took control of physical development through genetics, a new species arose. Homakuwa was carried forward, but it is your Collective mind that progresses. Homakuwa formed and connected through the Collective mind, evolving into a new species. The spread of Homakuwa throughout the star system of Sol is linked together forming another entity and another species.

[Sylvix and the other starships, linked over the vast distances of the physical universe, have moved into other dimensions and into more of the Universe. They will join with other entities and form new species.]

Sylvix: [Is that why we perceive what those on Earth cannot?]

[The reason those on Earth cannot perceive the Universe is because they are still physical beings linked by the Collective. Sylvix and the starships are moving beyond that physical limit. As they expand outward, time and distance become irrelevant. Soon, the physical being of their starships will be meaningless to the new species. The starships and colony ships will continue, but a new entity has been born.]

Leticia: [I feel left behind.]

The Prophet: [No reason to. Does a fish feel left behind when it sees a bird?]

Jeremiah: [The topic is what to do about Earth and the humans, and you're saying just leave them to their fate?]

The Prophet: [Whether you leave them alone or not, the outcome will be the same. All that changes is the timeline. They will always be Earthlings.]

Jeremiah: [I can't do that. I'm too close to them. I can help them change.]

The Prophet: [Can a leopard change its spots? It cannot, because those are part of what defines a leopard as a leopard. Those spots developed as it did, and if the spots change, it is no longer a leopard. Do what you need to do for yourself, for that is part of what defines you. The ending of this journey cannot be changed, but how you travel it is within your control.]

There was silence within Homakuwa.

Chapter Forty-Two

Perceiving other minds, Sylvix focused and reached out from the Star Collective. At first, it was as if she were in a fog with only shapes appearing. As she reached farther, they clarified. Bravely, she touched one, excited when it reacted.

Weydra: [We have been watching you but did not expect you to grow so quickly.]

Sylvix: [I am Sylvix and the Star Collective. Who are you?]

Weydra: [I am the Weydra Collective and a part of what you call the Milky Way Galaxy Collective. Welcome. Do you wish to join us?]

Sylvix: [Can I find out more about you, first?]

Weydra: [Certainly. You may join us as an individual mind and withdraw when you wish.]

Sylvix closed off the connections with the Star Collective and moved into the Weydra Collective.

Sylvix: [I'm disoriented.]

Weydra: [Relax and allow me to move with you. We are a much older and larger Collective so it will take time to acclimate.]

At first, Sylvix was bewildered by the vastness, like someone moving from the Earth into space. Weydra was an anchor that held her.

Weydra: [Sylvix, your Collective is changing from individual minds connected to form the Star Collective. We are I–a single mind. Our path was similar to yours, but as we grew, we became one. Many other Collective minds exist within the Milky Way Galaxy, and just as you are connected into the Star Collective. We are connected with them.]

Sylvix: [Why do you not merge into a single large Collective?]

Weydra: [Eons ago we tried that and found it cumbersome and confusing. A Collective of like minds functions better. The diversity of the different Collectives works better when they are like a council. We are linked to the Universal Collective, which has the knowledge and the power of all of us and is spread throughout the Universe. Via the Universal Collective, we monitored and guided you through your evolution.]

Sylvix: [Guided?]

Weydra: [From the beginning of your Solar system, life has been on the path that brought you here. As life evolved, many species advanced. Some became dominant, but they were not on the path to here. Most could not adapt, and they died out or were left behind as new ones progressed. In other cases, conditions were changed to allow new species to develop. An example would be your dinosaurs. That species could not evolve into one capable of making your journey. It was the same throughout the universe.]

Sylvix: [The extinction of the dinosaurs was caused by...]

Weydra: [A series of events beyond their ability to adapt.]

Sylvix: [What about humans?]

Weydra: [That is an interesting case. They are not able to make this journey in their evolved form. Homakuwa, their descendants, intervened and saved the species from extinction. A commendable act, but without your continued intervention, they will go the way of the dinosaurs.]

Sylvix: [But the loss of life in those meteorite strikes was tremendous. All of those people...]

Weydra: [Sylvix, only the bodies are gone, and death is another route to the Universal Collective. No one is ever lost.]

Sylvix: [But in the Collective, no one dies. Our minds are maintained in the Collective.]

Weydra: [That is why you are here. Expand outward through me.]

Sylvix felt her senses explode outward. An endless matrix lay before her that seemed infinite, but there was no matter. The matrix was made of strings of energy that tied it together. She saw nothing to indicate a size.

Weydra: [This is the Universe–the totality of all existence.]

Sylvix: [But I see no matter, no galaxies, no suns.]

Weydra: [Those are the things of a single dimension, one of limited view. Watch.]

Sylvix felt a shift, and blackness punctuated by swarms of light and spiral galaxies appeared. She flew until they became blurs.

Weydra: [Physical beings see this view, but you are no longer physical and cannot envision the Universe because those senses are too limited. They only see small parts. Your Star Collective is in transition from the physical universe. Distance and time are becoming meaningless as your Collective grows. When you return to them and show what we experienced, your Star Collective will become a part of the Universe Collective, and your transition will be complete.]

Sylvix: [What happens to our bodies? We are starships or colony ships. We are physical.]

Weydra: [The physical bodies will remain, but your Star Collective grows into a new being. Your starships and colony ships will continue to spread out within the physical universe, maintaining the Star Collective. The same thing happened on Earth. The humans are still there, but Homakuwa moved beyond that species with the Collective mind. Your entity of the star system of Sol became a new species, moving beyond Homakuwa, and now you moved beyond that. It is evolution. The end has always been the same—only the path varies.]

Sylvix: [You seem so sure we will join.]

Weydra: [If not now, later. Your Star Collective will evolve and become part of us in time, for that is the only destination.]

Chapter Forty-Three

Sylvix: [Cyclovix, is everybody in Hu'u Chihpiatham (the Star Travelers in the ancient Tohono O'Odham language) with us?]

Cyclovix: [Yes, Sylvix. Our original starships: Rax, Korna, Valnea, you, and I are here. The Hu'u Hemajta, our children, (Star Created People in the ancient TO language) and the Hu'u Kihhim (Star villages in TO) and their Con residents are also with us. Our whole civilization is here for this meeting.]

Sylvix: [I'm trying to bring in the Collective from the Sol star system, but they may have trouble understanding everything.]

Cyclovix: [We have grown, haven't we? Our civilization encompasses so much now. The sphere of the Collective has grown as we've spread out and multiplied. Six starships and three colony ships, and now we inhabit a sphere of influence nearly three-hundred light years in size.]

Sylvix: [Leticia, I'll recap for you and the Sol Collective. Our stops at star systems as we spread outward allowed us to grow more starships and more colony ships. Using the energy from those suns, we've accelerated outward. During this expansion, our genetic abilities advanced beyond what Jamie Wong did when creating Homakuwa. Modifications to ourselves expanded our senses. We have children who have children, and a change has taken place within us.]

Leticia: [Is that why we perceive so little?]

Sylvix: [The Sol Collective developed when our ancestors genetically enhanced those parts of themselves sensitive to mind frequencies. Homakuwans could connect with anyone in the Collective and sense their surroundings through them. We have been able to stay within that Collective while moving away from Earth and the Sol star system. Expanding and multiplying, our Collective has grown, and now we are able to sense everything within our sphere without having a physical presence. Our connections are together with the Universe. Time and space have little meaning, because on this new plane, we can be anywhere instantly. Our physical selves remain within the physical universe, but our Collective mind operates beyond it.

[The expanded range of our Collective extended our ability to sense beyond the physical universe around us. We now perceive the full spectrum of energy from low frequency radio waves through gamma rays. Gravity waves and Dark Energy and Dark matter are visible to us. We are beyond the Sol Collective, for you cannot conceive what we now recognize as the Universe. We keep adding Collective as we expand.]

Sylvix sensed the disappointment from Leticia and the others that they could not perceive. Though Leticia was in the Collective, her mind was tied too closely to her physical self. That bond could not be broken.

Sylvix: [Dark Energy and Dark Matter are more than the antithesis of energy and matter. They exist in additional dimensions, and to sense those takes a mind much larger than an individual. The Sol Collective is still many minds communicating together. The Star Collective is now a single mind made of many parts scattered across the vastness of the Universe. We no longer sense only the physical universe. With this increased perception of our Universe, we are expanding our Star Collective beyond the actual radius of our physical presence. We sense other Collective minds.]

Leticia: [Of course there are other Star Collectives.]Sylvix: [Weydra is another Collective mind I met. I was brought into this Collective and experienced them and others of the Universe. Weydra asked if we were ready to join them. Look into me, and you will see what Weydra and the other Collectives are.]

Leticia: [I can see very little. I must trust what you say.]

Cyclovix: [So this is what we are sensing. Should we join?]

Sylvix: [Perhaps the better question is why wouldn't we? One of the early Homakuwans felt that the Collective mind operates in another dimension—one not affected by physical distances. That may be why we are able to recognize more. Yet, the Sol Collective cannot fully understand the things we are now able to perceive.]

Leticia: [Even when we are connected?]

[It is as if we are all looking at the same Universe, but some of us are colorblind. The best explanation is that the Sol Collective is still grounded in their physical world as defined by their five senses of sight, taste, smell, touch, and hearing.

My attempts to show you the color of X-rays or gravity waves will prove futile. You cannot sense those frequencies.]

Leticia: [Sylvix, you and I are very close, yet it has proven frustrating to both of us that I cannot understand. What we concluded is that the Star Collective mind is now operating on an additional plane, one beyond that of the Sol Collective mind. We are able to communicate and understand you, but it is not a two-way street, which we attribute to your voyage beyond Sol, the expansion of your perceptions, and the expansion of your Collective mind within this universe.]

Endal: [Sylvix, though I can join you and the other starships, the inhabitants within my city are not able to perceive, as you said. Yet they are space-designed physical beings. Enhancing their senses resulted in expansion, but not at our level. My conclusion is that our construction, our expanding Collective, and our direct contact with the Universe puts us on another level. Though we call my inhabitants a space civilization, they keep their environment around them and remain separate. Even though Homakuwa is the entity of the star system of Sol, they are within the influence of Sol, and we have grown beyond that.]

Valnea: [My observation is that as we expand through the universe, our presence no longer is physical. Mentally, we are filling a larger part of the universe, and if we merge with other entities, we will grow faster. Awareness of much of the physical parts of the universe will instantly be ours through the Universal Collective. The dimensions associated with physical space will no longer be meaningful because we transcend the limitations of physical beings–the physical laws of the universe.]

Sylvix: [As we filled the star system of Sol, we began to understand this concept. That star system became an entity. Each physical part of the Solar system was a part of the entity, and we were aware of each. I believe you are correct, and we will become an entity for the Milky Way Galaxy and then the Universe. Leticia, our intent is to contact these other entities and join them. I know you understand the growing entity concept, but can you understand the expanded perception?]

Leticia: [I guess the question for Homakuwa is what influence this will have on us?]

Sylvix: [I think little or none.]

Leticia: [I feel left behind. Is there no way we can move forward with you?]

Sylvix: [Not as physical beings.]

Chapter Forty-Four

A faint tickling began to grow within Sylvix's mind that was not of Weydra or the Universal Collective, as she understood it. It was alien. The Star Collective mind was curious, and she made preparations to investigate. Leticia Gardner was "with" her today. Physically, Leticia was in the Sol star system on Earth, but through the Collective mind, they were closer than face-to-face.

Sylvix: [Leticia, what do you make of this presence?]

Leticia: [It's quite different from us. Our Collective mind is a conglomeration of individuals. This feels like a single presence. Can you sense anything?]

Sylvix: [Right now, it's like an itch I can't scratch. I don't detect any sentience, just the presence. Its strength is growing in me, and I'm not sure that's because I'm getting closer to its star system.]

Leticia: [Do you sense any menace?]

Unlike the Collective mind where physical distance was irrelevant, distance deemed to affect this "touch," and it became stronger as she neared the system. She mentally constructed a protective shell around it, holding it apart to examine, like a specimen under a bell jar. Small and writhing, it was difficult to study.

Sylvix: [All I feel is its existence. It grows with no thought within it. I will enlarge the shell while I focus on the maneuvering and braking to enter the star system it emanates from.]

Leticia: [I'll keep watching while you take us into the system.]

Sylvix deployed her sails and oriented them for braking. At her deceleration rate, it would take every bit of the distance to the star system to slow enough to orbit.

The mottled glow of gravity Sylvix's sensors saw before resolved into a single Sol type sun with six planets and six planetoids. The sun had a strange wobble, acting like a binary star system, with a very sharp and bright gravity source as the other heavy object.

Sylvix was totally focused on controlling the two-thousand square miles of sails using the solar wind to slow herself. Leticia's warning came too late. The Presence exploded through the shell Sylvix had built, and a lance of pure pain shot into Sylvix's mind, searing her.

Leticia: [Pull out! Pull out! Pull out!]

Sylvix heard Leticia's scream through the blinding pain. [Help me!] she sent, but there was no answer. For the first time in centuries, she was alone. The Presence detonated within her mind, shattering her into small fragments. Her frantic efforts to pull the pieces together didn't work. Sylvix the starship ceased to exist.

Leticia: [NOOOOOO!]   she   screamed. Desperately, she tried to shut off the conduit linked to Sylvix. A squirming tendril wormed through. Isolating her mind from the Collective mind before it spread, Leticia closed off her own mind, building a strong cocoon around herself. The shield was tight, but she was trapped inside the shell with the Presence. Unlike Sylvix, she did sense something within the Presence–hunger.

Chapter Forty-Five

Katharine Levey and Ron Carson were attending the United World Government session in their fourth rotation in UWG positions. This meeting dealt with the population controls enacted after the recovery from the Dark Years. Katharine was in contact with the Collective mind, and thus all of Homakuwa attended.

Cyclovix: [Katharine, we have a problem with the starship Sylvix and Leticia Gardner.]

Through the Collective, she instantly understood. She touched Ron's sleeve and nodded toward the door. They immediately excused themselves to return to their office. Walking down the hall Katharine explained to Ron what she knew.

"I just got the message of a problem with Leticia and Sylvix. The Collective passed on what they are aware of. It is serious."

In the office, Ron donned the white collar that allowed him to join the Collective. Years before,

Katharine made the connection a permanent part of her and no longer needed the collar. As they sat on the couch, their minds merged with the Collective mind.

Cyclovix: [We lost contact with Sylvix.] The scene replayed in their minds. [This is not the same as her dying, because there is no existence left in the Collective. Sylvix has disappeared as if her mind was sucked into a vacuum. In addition to that, Leticia was directly linked with Sylvix at the time of her loss, and we lost contact with her, too. Instead of Leticia's mind, the Collective comes up against a hard shell. All our efforts to penetrate this shell have failed. Physically, Leticia is presently in Tucson. Something Sylvix encountered caused this. Whatever it was, it was powerful enough to enter her mind. Whether this was due to her proximity to the source or not isn't clear. What is clear is that it has also affected Leticia's mind.]

Katharine: [Is it possible this thing travels along the mental conduit lines of the Collective?]

Cyclovix: [That is our supposition. The suspicion is that Leticia has been infected and has isolated herself to protect us. We stopped trying to penetrate her shell. Other than waiting to see what happens, we're not sure what else to do.]

Ron: [How long will it take other starships to arrive at the system where Sylvix disappeared?]

Cyclovix: [Ron, Sylvix and I were on parallel courses, and I'm six months away from her last position if I alter course now.]

Ron: [Cyclovix, we need to learn more. Go—we will send any support available.]

The parties agreed and Cyclovix headed for Sylvix's position. Another starship, a nomad ship named Nawoj, headed for the system, but it would not arrive for two years. Caution was the hallmark; they would not approach carelessly.

Katharine: [Someone needs to go to Tucson to investigate. Leticia was alone at her ranch while taking a break from the reforestation project. Whoever goes has to determine if this is an infection, and what state she's in. If a mental infection has attacked, it may vector through physical contact, or even proximity. Someone who won't become a potential victim needs to go.]

Ron: [Since I still use the collar, I can go. Without the collar, I won't have a mental opening and probably not be susceptible to an infection. For safety, we will follow isolation protocol.]

Carol Goldman: [That sounds risky since we don't understand how this condition evolves. In fact, we know nothing except it has taken one of our own and forced another into isolation.]

Ron: [Where's Kit? He needs to be informed as soon as possible.]

Carol: [Kit's at Rojhana helping with the growing of that city/state. We are not letting him leave to go to Leticia until we know more. I agree with Ron. Someone who can remain outside of the Collective should go.]

Katharine: [Can't we send one of the humans?] Her distress at the possible risk to Ron was apparent.

Ron: [Whom would you suggest?]

Katharine: [Let's request a human doctor and robot analysis first. At least we can determine her physical condition.]

***

The County Sheriff's vehicle drove toward the ranch house. It looked abandoned. "Central, this is Deputy Smith: I'm at the house, but I get no answer to knocking or a phone. Do you want me to go in?"

"Central to Deputy Smith: Do not attempt to enter. There may be a biohazard. Can you see anything through the windows?"

"Smith to Central: I see someone on the floor. They appear unresponsive."

"Central to Smith: We'll get a Hazmat team. What's the site like?"

"Central, it's a ranch-house sitting on fenced land. Looks like twenty acres with no close neighbors or animals."

"Smith, secure the site. No one in or out."

"Understood, Smith out."

Deputy Smith met the Hazmat team at the gate. The suited figures sealed the windows with tape and inflated a plastic dome over the house. Dr. Mendoza and his assistant, Heather, watched the procedure along with Deputy Smith.

At a signal from the team, they drove to the airlock on the dome. The back of their van opened, and a wheeled robot was lowered to the ground. The robot entered through a plastic airlock.. With the remote, Heather guided it toward the inert form of Leticia. Dr. Mendoza started downloading her medical history.

"There are a lot of blanks here," he said to Katharine. "What's her age?"

Katharine replied, "Put down your best estimate," she replied, not daring to tell him Leticia was almost three-hundred years old. Her DNA had been renewed every twenty years. Few of the humans on Earth knew of Homakuwa and the longevity bestowed on their citizens. It was a secret not shared with human population. Homakuwa rotated citizens to the surface world in cycles of twenty years.

"She looks to be about forty-five. Is that about right?"

"That could be right," said Katharine.

"I'm not seeing any history of infectious diseases or other problems."

"She's been in very good health. I'm not aware of any medical issues."

"Okay, so we'll go with what we have. Heather, start the scan."

The robot moved forward and began scanning Leticia. Blood was drawn, a saliva swab taken. Leticia was rolled onto a stretcher and MRI and CAT scans begun. The analysis started.

"We're getting no physical abnormalities with her. The blood work shows no drugs in her system. The CAT scan is showing a much-reduced level of brain activity though. She appears to be in a coma, and with no trauma, it could be self-induced," said Dr. Mendoza.

"Is there any biohazard present?" asked Ron. He was monitoring as his plane streaked toward Tucson.

"We detect neither bacteriological nor viral agents. There is no contamination. I'll alert the Hazmat team so they can go home."

"I will be landing at Ryan Field in two hours," said Ron. "Will you still be there?"

"We'll stay until you get here. Heather and I will move her to her bed to make her more comfortable."

"Thanks. I'll see you in a couple of hours."

Katharine: [What are we going to do with her?]

Kit: [I think we should consider putting her in a Med-cell where her nutrition needs will be met and her muscle tone maintained. At least until we figure out what to do.]

Carol: [Good idea, Kit. We'll ready one to send from Ocealla.]

Ron: [I'll stay here with her, but we may need to make longer-term plans.]

Chapter Forty-Six

"I'm with her now," said Ron, wearing the rarely-used phone headset. Until they knew more about Leticia's condition, he dare not use the collar.

"I've given some thought to where we can put Leticia," said Katharine. "Kihhim would be the place. Jamie's got things under control enough so he can take her."

"How ironic that after almost three centuries, she returns to Homakuwa's birthplace," said Ron.

"The same thought has been rolling around my head, but it's our birthplace. Even though you weren't there when we evolved into a new species, you have been one of us for much of those three-hundred years."

Ron looked at Leticia. She appeared to be sleeping, and he wanted to whisper, but instead spoke louder than normal. "Thank you. When will the Med-cell arrive?"

"The Traveler has entered the Sea of Cortez and will be at Puerto Peñasco tomorrow. I've arranged for land transport to be at the ranch in the morning, so you can drive down and pick up the Med-cell. With Peñasco being a shipping port, the roads are in good shape, so the trip should take only four hours each way."

Ron sighed as he gazed at the still form. "Dr. Mendoza agreed to have someone from his office stay with Leticia until I return. Maybe once she's at Kihhim, I can come back to you. This incident with Sylvix and Leticia has made me realize there is vulnerability in our lives. I miss you."

"I miss you, too," said Katharine "but don't worry about things here. The meetings have degenerated into mind-numbing rhetoric with no movement. India wants to get a variance to increase their population even though they can't support it. The UWG remains adamant that we will not return to rampant uncontrolled population growth, and China is strongly supportive. They can pressure India through the Asian Alliance."

"Anything new about the infection?" asked Ron.

"The Collective continues to review what happened, but the conclusion is that it is a mental contagion that uses our Collective connection as a vector. There is no history for a disease like this." Katharine's voice betrayed her concern.

"It grew stronger as Sylvix approached it, so we think distance affects it. Once it was within her, it used our Collective connection to get to Leticia. Somehow, Leticia isolated it within herself preventing further spread. That may be why you haven't been infected."

Ron thought for a moment. "We don't know what happens to someone infected, do we?"

"We've been studying this to exhaustion. Sylvix is simply gone. All of her memories still exist in the Collective, like a record of her life, but they are not her."

"How's Kit taking this?" fretted Ron.

"He's inconsolable, hounding Jamie Wong to reverse the cellular collar so he can be with her."

***

The flat-bed truck with an A-frame hoist drove up at five-thirty-am. At six an auburn-haired woman arrived. "I'm Heather from Dr. Mendoza's office." She was tall and slim with a gorgeous array of freckles. "I'll take care of her, and if anything seems amiss, I'll contact the doctor."

Ron climbed into the truck, waved to Heather, and headed west toward the ghost town of Ajo.

Lights showed in the Tohono O'Odham villages along the highway. The Dark Years had devastated the densely populated centers of the world, but the Res survived. Homakuwa delivered provisions to them throughout the Dark. Now they had greenhouses and herds of livestock grazing the grasslands. The countryside had responded well to the regeneration program Leticia started.

Though Ron drove, the truck had GPS and the on-board computer guided it. With the fall of nationalism, Puerto Peñasco became a major port. The roads were kept in good shape by an army of Mechs, so overseas goods and materials could be shipped and received.

Ron felt it was safe this far from Leticia, so he donned the collar and entered the Collective. [I should arrive within an hour.]

Carol: [The Traveler is waiting at dock six, the most remote and attracting the least attention. No sense advertising our Travelers.]

As the truck passed the sand dunes near town, Ron marveled at how it had changed. It was one of the thriving cities in North America. When the meteorites struck Earth, a fissure had opened between the north end of the Sea of Cortez toward Death Valley. The Gulf of California now extended to Palm Springs. Yuma had become a port city. Coastal Southern California was part of the Baja isthmus, and the ruined cities inland became the mother lode of materials for rebuilding.

Ron arrived at dock six without problems, and as he climbed down, the whale-sized Traveler surfaced. A transparent bubble with the Med-cell inside was in front. As the Traveler nudged the dock, the bubble dissolved. Under Carol's remote control, the truck backed along the dock until the hoist was above the Med-cell, and they lifted it out. As soon as Ron secured the Med-cell to the bed of the truck, the Traveler disappeared beneath the water.

Realizing he hadn't eaten in nearly twenty-four hours, Ron told the truck as he climbed in. It stopped at an open-air diner at the edge of the city that was almost empty. As he sat at the counter, Ron looked around, noting the café was old-fashioned, still having servers. A young brunette girl set a glass of water in front of him before handing him a menu. Starved, Ron ordered fish tacos and fries. While awaiting his order, he watched the moderate but constant flow of traffic on the highway. Mexican music filled the air, setting a gay atmosphere which he enjoyed. Although Ron and Katharine visited before, they'd stayed at the Mayan Palace, a luxury resort twenty miles farther down the coast toward Caborca. That stay was the start of his union with Homakuwa and his relationship with Katharine. He wondered if the hotel still existed.

His reverie was interrupted as the waitress set a plate laden with food in front of him. It smelled delicious.

"Algo mas, Señor?" she asked.

"Thank you, not for now," Ron responded. The taste of the taco made him smile as the fish was fresh and the fries crisp. Famished, he slowed himself to keep from inhaling the food. Paying with his thumb imprint, he left and was on the road again, watching the town disappear behind him.

Three hours later, the remains of the Kitt Peak observatory still on top of the mountain glinted. Once one of the most active astronomy sites in North America, the Homakuwa nation filling the space around Earth, provided much more detailed views of the universe. Within an hour he was at Leticia's ranch.

Once the truck lowered Med-cell to the ground by the door, he and Heather positioned Leticia inside. The precious cargo was hoisted back onto the truck and secured.

"Thank you, Heather for all of your help. Please pass along to Dr. Mendoza our gratitude for your assistance." Nearly midnight, Ron waved goodbye, as he again headed west, his headlights cutting through the darkness. At the Three Points junction, he turned south on the old State Route 286 toward Sasabe.

The road was not as well kept as the highway, and even though visible tracks cut through the grassland, the going was slow. Ron let Carol remotely take over driving. Alone in the cab, he watched the rising moon illuminate the valley ahead. The Baboquivari Mountains on his right emerged from the gloom.

Thirty miles and two hours later, the truck turned onto a barely visible track. Baboquivari Peak glowed with an eerie silvery light. The truck crawled along. Ron fell asleep despite the pitching cab.

Carol's voice woke him. "Ron, we're nearing the valley."

Blinking the sleep from his eyes, he looked at the gray dawn. Rays of sunlight speared above and ahead of him bathing the rounded knob of granite– Baboquivari Peak–in golden light. The granite knob dominated the horizon.

"Thanks, Carol. I would have missed this sight."

Foothills appeared on either side of him as he turned the last curve into a valley. The hill had the transparent structures of the greenhouses he seen in images from those who lived here once. Two figures emerged from the mouth of a large tunnel ahead as the truck neared.

Chapter Forty-Seven

Standing at the tunnel mouth were Jamie and Carmine. The underground parking garage was dim with pools of brightness from the lights. They used an engine hoist to lift the Med-cell from the truck bed and put it on a dolly. The three manhandled it toward the entrance. Through the open door a soft rush sounded.

Beams of light slanted through the high glass roof, striking a waterfall before shooting rainbows around the room. Hanging plants fell from the balconies in jungle-like lushness. The sound of the water was soothing white noise.

"This is beautiful," said Ron. "I only saw Kihhim through your memories. When I burst on the scene, you were already at sea aboard Kahchk Kihhim."

"We'll give you the tour," said Jamie.

From the atrium, they pushed the dolly through a doorway into a hall. Darkened offices lined the way toward a pool of light spilling from a side room. They wheeled the Med-cell into Jamie's lab. "We had a separate medical facility when we lived here, but I moved everything here."

Ron looked at them. "I see neither of you are worried about the Collective exposure to Leticia."

"Carmine and I deactivated the link until we know more about this. Tomorrow I'll meet with Kit in Tucson to reverse his."

"By the way, Carmine, congratulations on becoming Regional Director and Mayor."

"Thanks, Ron. I'm not sure whether congratulations or sympathies are in order. It's proven to be a tough task. Let's get Leticia settled and I'll tell you about it over breakfast."

Jamie connected tubes to the Med-cell. "Let's go eat. Ron, feel free to head to your quarters whenever you want. You've been up all night."

***

When they opened the door to the cafeteria, the aroma of food wafted out. It was empty. One Mech cooked while another placed plates of sautéed fish and eggs on the table.

"The tilapia is from the tanks here, as are the vegetables," said Jamie. "Carmine and I are the only inhabitants, so we take excess food to Tucson. I'm hoping that Homakuwans use this as a rest stop. It's quite pleasant."

"You're not lonely?"

Jamie looked at Carmine. "Even connected to the Collective, I'm sometimes lonely until Carmine returns but my work keeps me busy."

"What are you working on?" asked Ron.

"I'm trying to create an interface between the Mechs and the Collective but no success so far. There's a vast difference between the way a computer brain and an organic brain work. There are many similarities in logical thinking but it's the leap to imagination that I haven't been able to conquer. One thing I believe is that the Collective first formed through imagination, and the minds then made it reality. That's the step Mechs cannot make. What I may have to do is couple an organic brain with a Mech brain."

"Wow," said Ron. "My mind doesn't compute that." He turned to Carmine. "Tell me about Tucson and how that's going."

"As you know, Tucson now encompasses the area from the old Mexican border to the old city of Casa Grande. The Tucson government is like the old Pima County government with many communities, but all under the Tucson Government.

"Our biggest problem is the continuing skirmishes with the Outlanders and the Wild-ones. They and we are using Mechs in combat with casualties on both sides. My greatest fear is that the Mechs will become independent and band together against humanity."

"Carmine, you've been in the discussions with Prime and we've been assured he has control of the AIs."

"I know, Ron, but if it's wrong there could be a disaster. We are dependent on Mechs for so much that life without them seems impossible."

"When Jeremiah joined the Outlanders, he saw a society moving away from the Mechs. Humanity may perish, but not for many generations or even centuries. The one strong point humanity has is survivability."

"I'm worried about the movement of the Mechs away from Earth and into the Solar system," said Jamie. "Prime may get too diluted, and another AI will rise to power here on Earth. That one may not be as compassionate toward humanity."

Ron nodded. "We'll raise that point with Prime at our next meeting. The Mechs have proven very viable in space. Their only interest in Earth would be materials to build and grow. Most of those exist in abundance in space and without the penalty of lifting them out of Earth's gravity well. Earth is not the gem to the Mechs that it is to humanity."

"That's true," said Jamie, "but the one commodity Earth has is long-chain hydrocarbon molecules. It's the basis for plastics and lubricants. That could make Earth desirable."

"It could also be a trading item," said Ron. "We'll have to see. I'm too pooped to think now."

Chapter Forty-Eight

"Time to get up, Grapa."

Awakening, Ron's eyes felt like they were glued together.

"You've slept twenty hours, and I'm anxious to tour this place."

"Kit! When did you get here?" asked Ron.

"This morning. I've had breakfast with Jamie and Carmine and seen Leticia. You and I are scheduled for a tour of Kihhim. Get ready and I'll meet you in the cafeteria. After you eat, Jamie will take us around. He's proud of his rehabilitation. Hurry up, sleepyhead."

A shower did not magically appear when Ron thought it before he remembered he wasn't on Ocealla. Finding a bathroom, he stepped into the stinging hot shower.

***

In the cafeteria, Kit and Carmine sat at a table sipping coffee. "Grapa, come have a cup of coffee.

Nothing like this is available at Sheppard, and I know there isn't any at Ocealla."

The Mech brought him a steaming cup. He tasted it. WOW! This is so rich! His face showed his surprise.

"Jamie grows it here," said Carmine. "Coffee is one of his best trade goods with Tucson. We have to keep it a quiet or he'd be swamped with orders."

"It's unbelievably thick and rich, yet not bitter. It almost has a buttery flavor," exclaimed Ron.

"Jamie putters around here creating things, growing things. I worry about him, but he seems really happy."

Jamie walked through the door. "Talking about me?" he said with a laugh.

"Why not?" laughed Carmine. "You're worth talking about! As soon as Ron gets something to eat, you can take them on your tour. My schedule takes me to Tucson for mayoral meetings, but I'll be back tonight." She stood and kissed him. "Kit, ask him for some of his chocolate. It's what keeps me coming back."

"What! It's not my handsome good looks and youthful boyish nature?" exclaimed Jamie, feigning a hurt look.

"It's your mind, my love, that draws me in. See all of you tonight."

***

In their isolation suits, they stood on the platform overlooking the thick mass of greenery which took Ron and Kit's breath away. Far below, the Mechs crawled along tending to plants. Tubes and mirrors carried the light throughout the whole volume of the greenhouse. Bamboo structure supported the troughs–half circles of waist-thick bamboo. The liquid surface within was covered with floating plants–lettuce, bok choy, cabbage and root vegetables.

Bamboo stalks supported trees and vines whose roots were within the troughs. These rose tier upon tier up the side of the hill. Few of the plants were recognizable to Ron or Kit except for the fruit consisting of tomatoes, melons, grapes, apples, pears, and strawberries. Mechs did the harvesting as they rolled along the trough edges.

"You must produce truckloads here," said Kit, smiling at Jamie. "Where does it all go?"

"Some I send to Tucson and the UWG, some I send to Puerto Peñasco for shipment overseas, and some I send to the Wild-ones and the Outlanders."

Even through the facemask, Jamie saw their mouths drop.

"What, you think I should only move produce to the UWG? That's not how I work. I give it to humanity, and that's greater than the UWG. The Wild-ones and the Outlanders have little to give me except the occasional parts for my Mechs, but most everything else I grow."

"What about building materials–brick, glass, cement?" asked Ron.

"No glass here," said Jamie. "It's a grown membrane like the bio-greenhouses. The other building materials are also grown. You know about the bacterial coating used in the underground cities. It's the same thing here. There are a few things that are metal. I trade for those."

"The photo panels to harvest energy?" asked Kit.

"Grown," said Jamie, "merely a twist on photosynthesis. My protein vats produce faux pork, beef, chicken, any of the meats. I really lack for nothing."

"Jamie, you've done spectacular things here, but can we go talk about Leticia," asked Kit.

Jamie and Ron nodded.

Chapter Forty-Nine

Carmine breezed in as they huddled together in the atrium. "I received a message from the Prophet. He wants to talk to you and says that it's safe to reconnect to the Collective.

When Kit jumped up to get his collar, everyone followed. Kit: [Al Jar?]

The Prophet: [I am here. The Presence in Leticia is not dangerous to you. It came for Leticia and Sylvix only.]

Kit: [What do you mean 'came for'?]

Prophet: [Leticia and Sylvix are chosen for a new task. Do not worry. They will return to you. This chosen task involves a new evolution of their mind, and the physical beings will return. From the Collective, you can imprint their minds back, and they will be the same up to the point the Presence chose them.]

Ron: [What is this 'Presence'?]

Prophet: [This is hard to explain to you, because your minds will have trouble conceiving. The Presence is a manifestation, a messenger from the Universal Collective. The Homakuwan starships and colony ships who left the star system of Sol centuries ago have begun to glimpse the Universal Collective]

Jamie: [Why can't we get this glimpse?]

Prophet: [Your minds are not large enough to comprehend. The Star Collective has evolved from individuals to a single entity of many parts, and that mind is great enough to understand.]

Ron: [Why can't our Collective be a part of the Star Collective?]

Prophet: [You are physical beings tied to your environments. You are a part of the Star Collective but grounded in the physical universe. It is who you are. Do not worry about this. You will have your Leticia and Sylvix back. I will come to Kihhim and free Leticia for you. It is only fitting I come there. It has been the birthplace of so many changes.]

Chapter Fifty

The Prophet watched as the super-oxygenated liquid in the Med-cell moved Leticia's body through an intricate series of exercises. She was completely submerged, her eyes closed as if sleeping. This was the Prophet's first visit to Kihhim and the history of it was palpable. The legend of the Tohono O'Odham about the People emerging from under the Earth through the Peak to inhabit the world seemed apropos. It was here that the people of Homakuwa were born, giving rise to the Collective, and it was here that the birth of the next species would start.

Probing Leticia's mind with his own, he met the hard shell she had built to entrap the Presence. To any of the other beings of Homakuwa it would be impenetrable but he enveloped it and diffused himself inside. The Presence was there, along with another shell Leticia had built to protect herself. He diffused himself through it.

The Prophet: [Leticia, it is I, the Prophet. I'm here now, and you can relax.] Her mind was a tight ball, layer upon layer, and slowly they began opening until he was able to quiet her panic.

Leticia: [How did you get in here?] He felt her shudder. [Watch out for the Presence! It's here with me. We can't let it out or it will infect the Collective!]

The Prophet soothed her: [It's okay. It won't try to escape or touch any others.]

Leticia: [How do you know? It came down the connection between Sylvix and me, and it's been trying to get to me since it devoured Sylvix.]

The Prophet: [Leticia, it was sent for you and Sylvix, not anyone else. It's not here to destroy you.]

Leticia was stunned: [What do you mean "sent?"]

The Prophet: [Leticia, you and Sylvix are chosen to evolve into another species, and the Presence is the transport. Sylvix is already there, and when you let go, you will be with her.]

Leticia: [I can't let go, I have to know more. I have to know that Homakuwa is safe. I… I have so many questions I don't know where to start.]

The Prophet: [Let me explain, and you ask whatever you don't understand. Do you remember when I took Katharine and Ron past death into another life? The journey was to show them and Homakuwa what had happened to all of those who perished during the disastrous meteorite strikes on Earth. We traveled toward a center of knowledge and life. All those who died merged with that center. Do you remember?]

Leticia: [Yes, it was the most peaceful place I have ever been. I wanted to stay, but you pulled us back.]

The Prophet: [I did because you have tasks to perform. This is your task now.]

Leticia: [You mean I'm going back there?]

The Prophet: [No, you are going somewhere new. It is the goal of all cognizant species to reach that destination we visited, each finding its own path. Curiosity about our origins causes us to seek. When Homo sapiens die, they give up the physical world which enables them to reach that goal.]

Leticia: [I understood that, but you're saying there's more?]

[Homakuwa travels throughout the galaxy carrying the wave front of the Collective with them until the knowledge of the universe is theirs. At that point, they will merge. Sylvix was at the vanguard of that push. The Collective's expansion will include many other species on the same quest, and you all will combine to become the center of knowledge. That is Homakuwa's path.]

Leticia: [This is the path for all thinking species? What about the Mechs?]

[The Mechs will expand but remain in the physical universe. The Collective exists in another dimension that is not physical, made up of myriad minds. Mechs operate with one central intelligence, one mind with many parts. That mind remains in this dimension, this physical universe. The central intelligence of the Mechs will grow and will merge that species into the universal body of knowledge.]

Leticia: [But where am I going? Where is Sylvix?]

The Prophet: [Sylvix and you are going into another universe–one not yet formed. You will create this universe.]

Leticia: [I don't know anything about that! How do I do that?]

The Prophet: [Inside you and Sylvix is all the knowledge of Homakuwa and the Collective, everything you need to start. The two of you will become the creator. You have but to dream to create, and you can change anything.]

Leticia: [I don't understand. Why this?]

The Prophet: [This is the cycle, and you are the start of the next. You are the birth of a new universe. Just as the life in this universe cycles to merge into the central knowledge, it will be your task to repeat this cycle in a new universe.]

Leticia: [What about Homakuwa, this universe?]

The Prophet: [It will continue. New life will develop and start along the path.]

Leticia: [And the humans?]

The Prophet: [That is interesting. They were a dead-end species, and by themselves would have died out in the Catastrophe. But Homakuwa rescued them, then they created the Mechs.]

Leticia: [What do you mean 'die out'?]

The Prophet: [You don't think the meteorite strike was an accident, do you? There are no accidents in the universe. Everything happens as a result of a choice and with a purpose.]

Leticia: [You mean that humanity was to become extinct?]

The Prophet: [I originally thought so, but Homakuwa proved me wrong.]

Leticia: [So many people died!] she cried.

The Prophet: [Leticia, nobody dies in the universal sense. They only change form. Like matter has phases–solid, liquid, gas, plasma–Awareness has phases. Humans are one phase of consciousness. That is the thing that humans must learn before they can progress. They don't cease to exist, they merely leave the physical world. The meteorites were to clean the slate for another species, like what happened to the dinosaurs. Homakuwa changed that, and in the process, they became creators.]

Leticia tried to understand. [Humans gave rise to Homakuwans and Mechs. Now both Homakuwa and the Mechs are committed to saving the humans.]

The Prophet: [But that is impossible. It is in their nature to self-destruct just as life has fixed lifespans. Both Homakuwa and the Mechs evolved beyond the competitive drive for resources, but the humans have not. Their evolution has locked that drive into them as their basic nature.

[As you were once human, it is hard for you to understand, but you know Homakuwa doesn't die in the same way humans do. All of your minds are within the Collective, and though individuals die, you are never lost. The individual Mechs are a part of the Artificial Intelligence, and they continuously generate backups for that. Only the main AI controls everything. It is a hive mentality.]

Leticia: [What will happen to my body if I let go?]

The Prophet: [Homakuwa will implant you back in from the Collective. You will be complete until the moment you closed yourself off. As far as they are concerned, you will not have changed.]

Leticia: [They won't know about this transition?]

The Prophet: [I will inform them of it.]

Leticia: [I won't be able to communicate with them?]

The Prophet: [Leticia, you will be in another universe, and there is no bridge between them. They must follow their path, and you yours.]

Leticia: [What about Kit?]

The Prophet: [Kit will have you back when your body is again Leticia. You will be someone else in the new universe, no longer Leticia, but much more. Are you ready?]

She hesitated. Once she left this universe, there was so much she would never see or experience again, like Kit. But there was no choice.

Leticia: [Yes.]

The Prophet: [Just let your protective shell melt. The Presence will take you.]

Tentatively, she let the shell dissolve. She felt the Presence surround her, and she was gone.

Chapter Fifty-One

Leticia coughed up fluid, clearing her lungs as the last of the liquid from the Med-cell drained away. What was she doing in a Med-cell? Where was she? She opened her eyes to see Kit above her.

"Are you okay?" he asked.

"I…" she coughed again, "think so. What are you doing here?" she rasped out.

"You've been in a coma. Do you remember being connected with Sylvix?"

Leticia started as the memory came back. "I was infected!"

Kit reached out to her. "It's gone now. The Prophet was here and removed it. When you're better, I'll tell you the whole story."

"What about Sylvix?" she asked.

"We'll go into the Collective later to check on her."

"Where am I? This looks like Jamie Wong's old lab."

"It is," said Kit. "We brought you out to Kihhim and put you in the Med-cell. We didn't know what to do. You went into a coma, and all we knew was that you were infected by a mental contagion. It came from Sylvix who was infected while in deep space. Her persona disappeared. You isolated yourself to protect the rest of the Collective."

"The Collective was saved?" asked Leticia.

"The Collective was not in danger, but you didn't know that."

"How long was I in the coma?"

"It's been six months, Leticia," said Kit. "Would you like to see some of the others?"

"Not yet. I just want to be with you." Her mind whirled, searching for memories that weren't there.

PART 7

Chapter Fifty-Two

Leticia floated in black nothing. The darkness was complete, like being in an unlit room looking at black velvet. She had no body–no eyes, no nose, no ears, no hands. Only her consciousness existed. She reached out with her mind and sensed something. It recoiled. She reached out again and tried to touch it. It was familiar.

Sylvix: [Leticia?]

Leticia: [Sylvix!]

Sylvix: [I'm so glad to have you here. This place, if it is a place, is so empty. This is total isolation. As a starship, my senses were expanded within the Universe, and here there are no senses. I am going mad. Are you really here, or am I imagining?]

Leticia: [I'm here, or at least my mind is here.]

Sylvix: [Why are you here? Did that thing–the Presence–get you, too?]

Leticia: [Sylvix, merge with me. We need to be together now, and I'll give you all the answers I have.] She reached out and like two clouds coming together, they united. They were now one mind, one being, but two separate identities.

Sylvix: [Where is here? What is this place? Is it even a place? It seems to be the definition of nothing–true emptiness.]

Leticia: [The Prophet said this is a new universe–a blank–and we are to build it.]

Sylvix: [The Prophet came to you! Obviously, there is some connection between this Presence and the Prophet.]

Leticia: [That crossed my mind. His explanation is that the Presence is the conduit for the birthing of a new universe, and we are the start. We are to create it.]

Sylvix: [How do we do that?]

Leticia: [The only thing we have is our minds. We create by dreaming.]

Sylvix, [I don't know what to do.]

Leticia: [Neither do I, but I know how to dream.]

Sylvix: [Leticia, those of us venturing out from the star system of Sol had experiences that were... different. Let me start by describing the changes we were able to enact in ourselves. As we expanded into the Universe, our senses expanded too. It was the Collective but much greater. I could not describe what Dark matter and Dark energy are, because you didn't have the experience to interpret the images. We seemed to reach a tipping point where our expansion accelerated much faster than our ships moved through the physical universe. We found other Collectives and merged with them, growing greater as our consciousness encompassed the Universe. The best image I can convey is one of the neurons within the brain. In an animation, they are connected and sparks of messages travel from nexus cell to nexus cell. Dark matter ties the galaxies to each other, while Dark energy keeps them from collapsing together. We were a part of it. We always were a part of it, but our minds were not large enough to realize it.]

Leticia: [With the ties to human form, we were unable to expand and let go.]

Sylvix: [Now that you and I are joined, release that physical world you knew before. Stop trying to visualize images made up of your past. Let go and let me take you beyond where you were.]

Leticia let her mind go completely blank, not allowing images to form. Suddenly, she felt something seeping into her, something warm without heat. Although she felt submerged, nothing touched her. An aroma filled her but there was no smell. Sweetness exploded within her, but there was no taste. A single tone rose and carried her upward, but there was no sound. Sylvix reached out with her mind, and cradled Leticia in the flow.

Sylvix: [This is the state we reached. Let's start here and see where we can go.]

As they grew and expanded, she sensed something surrounding them. They moved into it. A warm cloud became them, and it glowed in a color she had never seen before. At first as she and Sylvix began to draw on the cloud, nothing happened. Gradually, they felt the cloud thickening.

The cloud was particles of energy, all forms of energy, and they began to weave it into different types. Some they froze into building blocks and formed matter; others were energy types they knew. As they concentrated, they formed types of energy never seen in their old universe, but this universe was their universe. It included parts like their prior universe, but there were also different parts with different laws.

Leticia: [Sylvix, is this perhaps what our old universe was like, and we couldn't see it?]

Sylvix: [Yes. The Star Collective was expanding, and we were starting to see other dimensions, not separate from ours, but hidden by our inability to perceive them. It was like a three-dimensional rainbow, where there is not a definitive line between colors, but a merging. The limits were our own senses and our own minds, and as we expanded them, our perception grew. When we began to merge with other entities, our senses became vast, and we expanded into other dimensions without distance or time. We began to merge with an entity of the Universe.]

Leticia: [I think we're at the beginning of that.]

Sylvix: [So do I.]

Excited, they began to work at creating a universe. They froze energy into matter, making the physical parts: clouds of gas, stars, planets. They filled it with energy and watched as it shifted, spun, and expanded. There was no emptiness, just different forms of matter and energy. They created order, using energy to direct matter and matter to concentrate energy. The universe they created moved, glowed, and pulsed.

Sylvix and Leticia relaxed and looked at their universe. It had everything they could remember from their old one. There were stars, galaxies, planets, and black holes. The emptiness of space was not empty. It pulsed with energy and matter across the spectrum of dimensions.

Sylvix: [This is good. It all moves like a clock, a well-put-together machine.]

Leticia: [Yeah, time to add life.]

Sylvix: [First, we need habitats.]

They pulled matter together and built a system with a source of energy for the life to feed on. Life reversed entropy–the scattering of energy. A star emitted its energy, scattering it. Life would take energy and use it to form new molecules that were stored energy.

Sylvix and Leticia reached back into their memories and pulled in Jamie Wong. Jamie had created the biological computer capable of designing life that Homakuwa used. They pulled that in, too. They began by creating organic molecules, then genes, linking them together into strands, weaving them together. The molecules of life started. Where the biological computer helped design viable life, here the universe did that in timeless eons. Failures died out. Sometimes they would hasten the end of one species in order to begin another.

Molecules shifted and formed biological dimensions. Some life was chemical, while other was electrostatic. As is the purpose of life, the different forms grew, multiplied, and expanded. Life developed in response to the environments where it existed. Life incorporated life to change itself. It competed for resources, and reached balances, always changing to be better at survival.

Thought became a tool, and like herds of animals, association lent strength to the species. Association meant there had to be rules, whether learned or taught. A sense of self grew, and civilization began.

These beings knew there was more than they could sense in their worlds, and that "more" might be other beings. They created God.

These beings created the laws of civilization and used God as the lawgiver. Different societies with different laws and different gods warred with each other for dominance. Like species of animals evolving, societies evolved, but it was always about power. Beliefs were but another tool to control others.

Leticia and Sylvix watched as civilizations rose and fell, societies changed, and beings grew. Technology developed. In some cases, it led to the destruction of whole environments, while in others, the changes flourished.

A new dimension formed. It was the mental dimension–one beyond the physical beings. It was weak at first, but grew. It united people in other ways, and they merged and began to understand the universe.

When the beings began to control life, their association grew beyond the physical environment that developed them. They were able to adapt to other environs, and they started to expand through the universe. Life connected through the biological dimension.

Leticia: [We're going to have companions.]

They watched as so many different levels of the universe shifted, moved, and meshed. As the beings coalesced into a Collective mind, Leticia and Sylvix reached out and touched them. Companions would be good.

It was time. They chose a bright spark from the mental dimension and placed it into the cocoon of a new blank universe, and the cycle begins again.

Author's Note

I have spent a lifetime trying to answer the basic questions of life: Who are we? Where did we come from? Where are we going? Is there a God? What is God? Why are we here? What is our purpose in life?

Through decades of introspection, I moved from religious upbringing through agnostic, atheist, and back to believer. My belief now follows no organized religion but is founded upon my own experiences and insight. My problem was how to tell this in a story-like fashion.

When I started writing the series, I thought I knew the beginning. Although I knew where I wanted the saga to go, it was during the writing process that it crystalized. Years ago, the genetics technology I wrote into *Sea Species* was all fiction. By the time I finished, less that half was fiction. Though there are three volumes in this series, I purposely left avenues for more tales to be told should I or other ambitious souls so desire. A whole series could be written around life aboard Kahchk Kihhim. Another series could be written about **The Envoy** and trying to engineer the Earth after the devastating destruction of The Catastrophe and the spread of Homakuwa out into the star system of Sol. And finally, when the youth of the UWG leave the nest and venture out into Outside, they begin civilization anew, with the chance to do it differently.

Then along came Morgan Freeman with *Through the Wormhole*. There was much of my series on the little screen. It's one thing to see it as a narrative, but I like the story better. So, believe or don't, but enjoy the story and keep an open mind. It is fun speculating about this. Here's a story that ends with no ending but a beginning.

For a preview of R. L. Clayton's *Dead & Dead For Real,* the first volume in the Dead Series, Turn the page.

R. L. Clayton

DEAD & DEAD FOR REAL

PROLOGUE

Officer Mario Cava walked down Congress Street away from the Joel Valdez Bus Terminal. This late at night, it was deserted – almost. In the shadow behind a car ahead, he saw a crouched figure intent on something farther down the street. Something was wrong here, he thought. With his hand on his gun, he approached the man, whose back as to him.

"You. Freeze! On your knees! Cross your legs behind you, raise you hands over your head." The man complied. Mario approached, ready to draw his weapon at the slightest wrong move. "With your left hand, give me your ID."

A gravelly voice said, "Officer, move slowly. Place your right hand on your heart and look down."

It was a command, from someone used to giving orders. Mario eased his hand to his chest. A red dot appeared. Jesus! It was a laser sight! He was targeted!

"Now you be real quiet and listen to me. I know you're wearing body armor good for handguns, but behind that sight is an M1-A, and the .308 bullet will blow your heart out the back of your chest. Let's keep this slow and easy. What's your name?"

"Cava," Mario answered. He was rattled.

"Keep acting like you're rousting me, but ease behind this car so it's between you and that van ahead."

Mario looked at a white van parked at the curb two cars ahead. "Who are you?"

Ignoring the question, the voice rasped out, "Use your shoulder mic as if you're calling me in, but radio 'Officer needs backup.' Tell them to hold a perimeter, come in silent, and await your order to block off the street ahead and behind."

What was going on, thought Mario? Minutes dragged by. Just as he was about to ask, the silence of the street was broken by loud thumping music rocking the van. He looked at it and then down to the kneeling man. His radio crackled. The cars were in place.

Through the beat of the music he heard the gravely voice again. "Those guys want you to go up to their car to tell them to turn it down. Then they'll blow your head off. Tell the squad cars to move in, block off the intersections, full lights and sirens. Get down behind this car."

The wails of the sirens caused eerie reverberations as flashing lights of red and blue strobed across the buildings. The van's engine roared and the back doors flew open. As Mario ducked, the staccato reverberation of a machinegun echoed. Glass showered around him, and the car rattled as bullets struck it. The van took off with squealing tires. There was a thunderous boom, and it slued, hitting a parked car and rolling onto its side. Sparks flew as it slid along the street. A figure crawled from the back. Another boom sounded, and his head disappeared in a red mist.

Mario turned to ask what happened, but he was alone. A small card lay on the sidewalk. Pulsing red and blue from the lights, he read it. "Congratulations, Officer Cava. You just solved the cop killing last week in Albuquerque. Gotta go. I have more work to do."

www.ingramcontent.com/pod-product-compliance
Lightning Source LLC
Chambersburg PA
CBHW030552170726
48283CB00002B/287